THE GHOST OF EMILY TAPPER

NITA ROUND

Edited by
KRISTA WALSH

Cover Design
MAY DAWNEY

Copyright © 2021 by Nita Round

All rights reserved.

The right of Nita Round to be identified as the author of this work has been asserted by her in accordance with the Copyright, Patents and Design Act 1988.

No part of this book may be reproduced in any form or by any electronic or mechanical means, including information storage and retrieval systems, without written permission from the author, except for the use of brief quotations in a book review.

The characters, incidents and dialogue herein are fictional and any resemblance to actual events or persons, living or dead, is purely coincidental.

Dedicated to:

Readers everywhere

New Book Edition

This is the latest version of The Ghost of Emily Tapper, produced with Pink Tea Books. The story has been rewritten in parts, new scenes added, and extended in others.

1

TICK TOCK

In the kitchen of Magwood Hall, Maggie Durrant stood before the cooking range and waited for the water in the kettle to boil. Her thoughts, however, were focused on any place other than the here and now.

Steam rose through the spout, the whistle shrieked for attention, and she snapped out of her thoughts long enough to take the kettle off the heat.

She looked up at the age-worn clock, its craquelure fascia discolored from a long and extended life in the kitchen. The reassuring sounds of the ancient timepiece echoed through the cavernous kitchen and marked the passing of each minute with mechanical exactness.

Maggie paused. She breathed out a long gust of steam and shivered in the sudden chill.

Tick. Tock.

The clock drew her attention again and all thoughts of tea vanished.

Tick.

The spring mechanism groaned and strained as it reached towards its next movement. Time lengthened and stretched like elastic, almost to the point of breaking.

Tock.

The moment ended and reached for the next.

Tick.

Maggie, aware of the nuances of her clock, stilled her mind and her body. She waited for the clock to announce its next movement, and yet she knew it would not.

Time took a deep breath and held it. It was neither then, nor now, but caught *between,* and she knew this instant well. The moment expanded and stretched, until this instance was everything. She had been warned, now she needed to see what surprises lay in store for her this time.

Maggie attended to her world with the fullest extent of her senses. The chill of her skin was warmed by the heat radiating from the solid fuel stove. The lingering aroma of chicken pie wafted up from an oven door left ajar. Her clothes grew heavy and clung like silken chains to her body. She strained to hear more beyond the confines of the kitchen, as if she could improve her ability by force of will alone. Her mind grew focused, and the mundane fell away to leave a quiet stillness in which she could seek further clues or details beyond the mundane. Then she heard the whispers, the echoes of a voice long dead. These muted words had no place in this world, and yet they reverberated through the corridors of Magwood Hall as though they had always been there—and in some sense, they had.

She focussed now on sounds that were closer. The old fluorescent lights fizzled and buzzed. The gas burners on the stove hissed a warning, and she closed the gas taps and cut the open flame. Wind rattled the kitchen windows with such vigor, she thought they would break.

The whispers quieted.

Somehow that seemed worse.

She looked rapidly from left to right, but she saw nothing. At first. A shadow at the very edge of her field of view flashed by, and Maggie took another step backward. A steel pan flew from the top shelf and crashed to the floor at her feet. Maggie sighed, picked up the pan, checked it for damage, and placed it on the kitchen table.

Tock. Time breathed out.

"I know you're there. It is not my time yet," Maggie said.

"Dooo yooou?" a voice echoed. *"Do. You?"*

"No," Maggie answered.

A chill breeze blew around her shoulders and wrapped her skin in bitter cold. She shivered in spite of herself.

"Do you?" the wind asked once more.

Maggie slammed her hand on the table. "No. You know I don't. Why don't you leave me alone?"

A sigh, like a heart broken afresh, breezed through the kitchen. Then it was gone.

The whispers stopped, the kitchen was a kitchen, and Maggie knew she was alone once more. "It is still not my time," she shouted, even though no one stood nearby. "Not my time. You hear?"

Tick.

She leaned against the table, head down, and defeat weighed upon her shoulders. "Damn," she said. She grabbed the pan and poured hot water into the teapot. "You're going to drive me insane before you kill me, aren't you?"

Tock.

Maggie scowled. She needed no one to remind her that time was running out. She finished making her tea and strode with such determination from the kitchen that the china cup rattled in its saucer. Behind her, the antique clock once more marked the passing of the minutes with mechanical and age-worn exactness.

Tick. Tock.

OH, BROTHER!

Maggie placed her tea on the side table next to her usual and favoured seat. She ignored the man who sat in the chair to the far side of the inglenook fireplace, and stood right in front of the open fire. Even though the Great Hall was already warm from a generous pile of burning logs, the ice in her bones needed more than mere flames. She rubbed her hands together against the heat and stared into the fire.

"I hear you crashed the Land Rover. Again," her brother, Charles, said.

She didn't turn to look at him, but simply said, "Yes." After the episode in the kitchen, talking to anyone, her brother in particular, was not something she relished.

"It costs money, you know, to repair vehicles every time you break them. You can't go around wasting my money."

"Your money?" She rubbed her fingers across the top of her chest where the marks of the seat belt were still raw underneath her shirt. Anger blazed and overrode the pains of her body. She closed her eyes and tried to regain control of her emotions. Anger never worked with her brother; he would use all emotions against her. "I didn't plan on having an accident."

"What was it this time?"

"Excuse me?"

"What did you do to cause the accident?"

"I did nothing. The brakes failed."

"Again? Your driving is not improving, is it?"

"This has nothing to do with my driving. It was a mechanical problem, and the brakes simply malfunctioned. I wonder how something like that could have happened."

"You should take more care."

"I do, but sometimes I wonder if it wouldn't matter whether I took care or not."

Charles snorted. "Sounds like paranoia creeping in. Well, with you it is not so much creeping as galloping."

"Ha ha. You are so very funny. Sometimes I can barely contain my mirth."

"No need to be so sarcastic. You are becoming rather mistrustful, dear. Perhaps now is the time to go and see a doctor or something."

"I don't need a doctor. Besides, even if I am paranoid, it doesn't mean there isn't someone out to get me. Philip took a look at the damage, and he thinks the brake line was cut."

"Locals! What does he know about such things? Does he claim to be some great forensic expert now?"

"He claims nothing more than what he is, and what he is, Charles, is a mechanic. He knows what he's talking about. More than I can say for you." She shrugged. "I'm fine, by the way. Thank you so much for asking if I was injured in the crash."

"Don't be facetious. I can see you're fine. You're standing here giving me lip."

"Sometimes I think if it weren't for the fact you are my brother, I should have you escorted off the estate."

"But I am your brother, dear sister, and if this were all mine, which it should be, I would marry you off and run the estate in a very different manner."

"How very medieval of you. Still, you can't marry anyone off against their wishes."

"Oh, I think I could. I just need the right incentive to make someone take you off my hands."

"No, you couldn't."

He sat there and smirked.

"It'll be yours soon enough," she said.

Now he snorted in disdain. "Please don't tell me you are listening to those old wives tales as well." He shook his head slowly. "Seriously, sister mine, even if it were true, I'd still have to wait, and in the meantime, I'd rather you did not waste my inheritance."

Maggie closed her eyes and tried not to let his words bother her. "Never mind. Even if you took control tomorrow, you could never manage the estates." She knew her brother well, and Charles was not the kind of man to take an active part in anything to do with their estate. "With you at the helm, as it were, you would bankrupt us all within weeks."

"I would manage."

"Would you?" She didn't think he would. "You should help out more."

"What on earth for?"

"To show that you understand the estate, and to help pay for those very fine clothes you wear."

"I understand everything perfectly well, and these clothes are my right. Why would I want to get them dirty?"

Maggie wondered the same thing. Charles didn't own work clothes of any kind, but he did possess the finest Italian leather loafers, which would never see the inside, or the outside, of a working barn. She stared at his shoes and longed for a day when she could wear or own such luxury. Her finest rubber boots were waterproof as long as she remembered to renew the duct tape keeping them together, and her waxed jacket, with the almost non-existent quilted lining, was all the protection she had from the rain and cold. In the mountains and valleys of her estates, it rained often, and when it didn't rain, the air was cold and damp. "Therein lies the difference between someone who can work the land and someone who would bleed it dry."

He sighed in such a way to make her feel his scorn. "Our line is an old one, and it deserves more than this. Only fools would work when there are plenty of farmer tenants to do what needs to be done. The purpose of life is pleasure and joy, not the folly of being knee-deep in animal excrement."

"You sound like a character in some dramatic opera."

"Still, I am not wrong."

"And if I don't work who will pay your trust money? The amount you get paid has very little resemblance to what the estate can pay."

"Not my problem. The trust is my right."

"Perhaps destitution would be a better option for us all, then."

"I think we are far from such distastefulness."

"I wouldn't count on it, but never mind, eh? It will be yours soon enough."

"Of course." He smiled, but there was neither warmth nor humor in his shark-like leer. "Still, you're the *heir* and you're in charge." He folded his paper, placed it on the side table, and rose in one fluid motion.

She wanted to snarl at him. Only her brother could make 'heir' sound like something dirty.

"Never mind," he said. "I bet you're looking forward to your birthday, seeing as it is destined to be your last one."

"I thought you didn't believe in the old lore and the curses of the peasants."

"I don't, but you do. Will you do something special on this

momentous occasion, or will you celebrate in your usual fashion—alone, with a glass of wine?"

"What's it to you what I do?"

"Nothing. It's one birthday closer to my inheritance. Nothing more."

"You're a heartless bastard," she growled.

"If I am, so are you," he replied.

She shook her head. "I take it you're not going to assist on the farm tomorrow?"

"Don't be silly. Why would I want to do such a thing?"

"To help out?"

"Honestly, sister mine, if you want to make money, you should turn it into a theme park. I would, and I'd make a bloody fortune."

"Over my dead body."

"Exactly that." Charles laughed. "For now, it's your inheritance, dear sister. You deal with it. And try not to crash any more vehicles. I'd rather you didn't leave me penniless."

Maggie scowled; it was one of her most common expressions around Charles.

"I'm off now. Don't wait up for me, I'll be late. Very late."

"Where are you going this time?"

"I'm going out to act like the lord you can never be."

"Being the lord of this estate is about more than flaunting position and wealth, especially when the wealth is not yours."

"Not mine…yet. But I will flaunt my privileges, as you put it, with all the enthusiasm I can muster."

"You're a prick, Charles."

"Is that the best insult you have?" He grabbed himself and smirked. "At least I have one, which makes me the man of this pile. As one, I should be in charge."

"Must you be so crude?"

"When it amuses me, yes, and so far it amuses me immensely. After all is said and done, I will be the one to continue the Durrant line. You can't do that—or won't—so my role in life is clear."

"Go then. Get drunk, find some strumpet, and I hope she gives you a nasty itch for your troubles."

"Maybe you should go find yourself a strumpet. It might put a smile on your face."

"Get out!" she roared.

Charles laughed as he left. "Don't forget to go and milk the hens, or whatever it is you do at dawn. Looking at chicken eggs is as close as you'll ever be to getting laid."

"Crude, Charles. Very crude," she responded, although he was no longer in the room. She slumped into her chair and stared into the fire. Her anger did not last long. What was the point? Anger changed nothing. No matter what she did, she couldn't change a thing.

Charles would be the next Lord Durrant, he would have children, pass along his vileness, and the cycle would continue. There was no point fretting about the things she could not change. The title made them feel entitled, it seemed. The Durrants were a family destined to perpetuate all the bad attitudes associated with old money. They never seemed to learn.

She stared at the fire until she heard the back door slam closed. A few minutes later, she heard the roar of Charles' gas-guzzling sports car as he raced out of the courtyard and through the gate.

Alone at last, Maggie settled into her chair by the fire and allowed herself the chance to relax. The stress of the day seeped from her muscles. Heat from the fire bathed her skin, and the warmth spread throughout her body until the chill in her bones fled.

For a moment, even though her world was a harsh and unforgiving one, she felt at peace, almost content. She worked hard, and although she had no time for play, she didn't miss the frivolity that others took for granted. Her only wish, if she could have one, would have been the chance to share at least some of her life with someone.

She closed her eyes, and a face appeared in her mind's eye. It was not a new image. The same face had haunted her dreams and thoughts since she was a child. Brown eyes, so dark they appeared almost black, looked at her with cool disdain. Tapper eyes, they were, and the face of her fate was a beautiful one.

Maggie wondered, as she stared into those imagined eyes, where in the world this Tapper woman lived. Did this unknown Tapper dream of her too? Did she know they would meet? What would this Tapper heir make of her, the Durrant heir? She wondered, too, if her father had also dreamed of his Tapper nemesis? Did he need to dream of her when his Tapper, Maud, lived so close they could hate each other by sight?

Maggie shook her head and tried to clear away her thoughts. Given the history of the two families, the one with the dark eyes wouldn't care at all.

M aggie woke with a start. The fire had long since gone out, and even the last embers of the fire had no more heat. A chill filled the air, and not only because the fire had gone out. She shivered in the cold. Steam jetted out of her nose and mouth and goosebumps erupted along the length of both arms.

"Damn," she muttered.

In the distance, whispers echoed through the quiet of the night, and they were growing closer. She looked at her watch: fifteen minutes past midnight. Right on time.

"Do you?"

She heard the question as clearly as if someone spoke at her shoulder. Yet when she peered behind her, no one was there. There never was, no matter how often she looked.

"Do you?" the voice persisted.

Maggie shook her head. Why bother with a response? Her answer never changed, and even if she said something, it would never appease this spirit.

"All is lost."

"I know," Maggie whispered back, "I know."

3

CAR DAMAGE

Maggie left the hall a little after dawn, and when she arrived in the farmyard, she was gratified to find Phil Jackson waiting.

"Fixed it?" she asked as she pointed at the Land Rover.

"I have. Looked worse than it was. You drove well considering where you crashed it."

"Luck, I suppose, and caution. I never travel fast around the Inger. There are too many bends and not enough barriers. Any other mountain road, and I probably wouldn't be here to talk about it."

He nodded. "So, I straightened the panels, but it'll be a while before I can spend the time painting them. I'll brush rather than spray if it's all right with you. It'll be quicker."

"Sure. It doesn't have to be pretty, just functional."

"As I thought. In the meantime, I've primed and undercoated any exposed metal to help stop the rust until I can put on a good coat of paint. Probably next week if that suits?"

"Excellent job. Thanks, Phil."

"No problem."

"And did you manage to get a look at the brakes?"

"Do you want my opinion?"

"Of course I want your opinion."

"Then I'd say they were cut. But you should get an expert in to check. Their judgement would be more certain and reliable."

"You're reliable, and I trust your judgement."

"For you, but the police would want to be more certain."

"If the brakes were cut, I can't blame it on the ghosts, then?"

"Not unless ghosts use tools."

"That doesn't make sense."

"I'll show you the tool marks if you like."

"No, it's okay, Phil. As I said, I trust your judgement. You've never let me down."

"You ought to see this with your own eyes anyway." He led the way to the back of the Land Rover and picked up a few pieces of piping laid out on the tail gate. "This is the pipe section I replaced. Good job you have the Mark II—it's almost an antique, but at least they're made to be fixed in the field. I had spare copper nickel pipes in the workshop, so it wasn't a difficult job to bend it to shape. The fixings were a bit of a bugger, but we can't have everything." He pointed to a shiny part in the middle of the grease and dirt. "Anyway, here you can see tool marks through the grease."

"The shiny part?"

"Aye. Metal doesn't shake off grease and dirt all on its own."

She peered at the marks. "Pliers do you think?"

"Maybe. Something like it anyway. Enough to pinch it off and waggle it about a bit."

"Why?"

"Well, if it was just copper, you could pinch it closed. That would deform it enough to block the flow, which would be a nuisance at best. Or it would help to see if there were signs of

13

corrosion and give it a pull in case. That would also break the pipes."

"Ahh," she said.

"It wasn't just the lining section you see there. I saw a flexi-hose had been cut through. Now, I replaced that particular hose with a reinforced mesh one a month ago. That is not going to break on its own."

"Is there any chance this is one of those times when it just wears out and breaks?"

"Any one of these things on their own? Maybe. But not when the brake lines have been severed in two places to make sure. With no brake fluid to the calipers, the brakes won't stop you. As you discovered." He looked her in the eye. "This is no accident. My guess is someone doesn't like you."

"It looks that way, doesn't it?"

"Will you call the police?"

"And tell them what?"

He looked thoughtful for moment. "I suppose you're right. Keep them out of town business. Anyhow…" He stared off across the hills. When he rolled his shoulders, Maggie knew he had more to say.

"Mrs Jackson asked me to mention a few things," he said after a while.

"How is your wife?"

"Doing well, thank you for asking."

"Is there a problem?"

"Did you know Arthur Wainwright was taken to hospital the other night? Looks like a heart attack."

"No, I didn't know. How is he?"

Phil shook his head. "I am not sure, but the wife thinks it's not good at all."

"I'll go see Mrs. Wainwright later, she must be in a terrible state. Is she at the hospital?"

"Aye. Visiting hours are three until five."

"Anything else?"

"My wife wants to know what you were going to do with old Maud's place." He looked discomforted. "It's a shame to allow such a nice house to go to waste when there are people here in need."

"Like your son?"

"Like my son, his wife, and a little one on the way," he admitted.

"Congratulations."

"Shame there's no place for them to go."

"I'm sorry, but I can't help. I can't build more houses for you."

"What about Maud's house? It's empty now that she's gone. You can do what you like with it."

She smiled. "I wish I could, but it isn't my house, Phil. Maud owned it."

"What! Owned it? You're joking."

"Don't look so shocked. The Tappers have owned the house since long before I was born."

"So if you sold off one house, will you sell off any more of the estate houses?"

"No, Phil. I have no plans to sell any of the other estate houses."

"Folk will be happy to hear their homes are safe, but what of Maud's house?"

"It forms part of her estate and will be held for her kin."

"Maggie, you know as well as I do, Maud Tapper had no kin. No kin at all."

"Perhaps she didn't," Maggie muttered, but a vision of deep brown eyes filled her view. "But there is a Tapper out there."

He thought for a moment. "Have you met her then, the young Tapper?" Not even the slightest consideration the Tapper would be a man.

"No."

"You know it for sure?"

Maggie nodded.

"To be expected with your history. If you pay attention to the world, it'll tell you what's coming."

"Yes. We'll know more soon enough."

"Aye, we will." He nodded. "And how will you feel, your history with the Tappers being as it is?"

Maggie shrugged. What could she say?

"My apologies. It is not my place to talk about such personal matters." He scrunched his eyes. "It would have been better if there were no more Tappers. You could put the past to rest at last, and mayhap there would be peace for a change."

"I don't think issues like ours can be fixed. It will take time and a great deal of effort."

He shrugged. "It is what it is. Maggie, you will do what you can."

"I will."

"Meanwhile, is your brother coming to give us a hand? There be lots to do and not enough time to do it all."

She shook her head. "I'm not sure it's worth asking the question anymore."

Phil chuckled. "Always worth asking. You never know."

"Not in this lifetime, Phil. Not in this lifetime."

4

EMMA

As far as Emma was concerned, Marcus Riley was the biggest prat on the planet. Alas, he was also her boss, and he never let her, or anyone else, forget it.

"Emma," he bellowed from an office a mere thirty feet away. "My office."

Barbara, who sat at the workstation opposite, rolled her eyes. "Oh, look. It's your turn for his delicate attentions."

Emma snorted, and she didn't care whether he heard her or not. She got to her feet anyway. "I'm coming," she grumbled. She gathered pencil and paper because he often liked to treat her as his personal secretary rather than the Creative Director she was supposed to be.

"He's got someone in with him," Barbara whispered as Emma walked past her desk. "Looks like an undertaker. I bet you'll be the one to write some dreadful commercial about coffins."

Emma snickered. "Anything would be better than bloody stupid ads for spray cheese."

"Yes," Barbara grinned. "You could always tell him, you know, being a media company involves more than selling shoddy jingles and running dubious ad campaigns for things no normal person would buy."

"Right. You'll get me fired, and unemployment is what I don't need right now."

"He hates you anyway. Unemployment is a tantrum away."

"Don't I know it." Emma stopped where she stood. "I wish his father was still alive. Maybe we could get back to what we're good at."

"Don't hold your breath. Marcus is a fool and he's not going to change any time soon."

"You're right, of course, but I have a mortgage, and I don't fancy looking for a replacement job."

"Maybe you should sleep with him. It would keep him sweet at least."

"Barbara!"

"Well, you never know."

"What I do know is that you have a warped sense of morality."

"Yes. And look where it has got me."

"Married with three kids and a husband who adores every step you take."

"Dreadful, isn't it?" Barbara grinned. "Jealous?"

"Of course." Emma chuckled as she strolled across the office to Marcus' door. No matter how loud he yelled, she sure as hell was not going to give him the satisfaction of rushing. She stopped in the open doorway. "You called?"

Barbara had been right. The visitor, a tall man in a long dark coat, stood ramrod straight in the middle of the room. Marcus, in his expensive leather chair, looked ill at ease, and his reaction was odd in itself.

"Come in, Emma." He beckoned her inside. "Close the door behind you. This is Mr Schilling."

"Excuse me, Mr Riles," Mr Schilling interrupted. He was a

soft-spoken man, and his voice was little more than a whisper.

"Mr Riley." Marcus frowned as he repeated his own name, as though he needed a moment to decide whether he'd been insulted or not.

"Of course, Mr Riley, but this is a private matter."

"It is private here."

The tall man nodded. "This is a private matter for the ears of myself and my client only. It need not be in this office, so if you could point me in the direction of a suitable location, I'll be out of your way."

Client? Emma wondered.

Marcus stared at him and then at Emma. "I'll be in the main office in case you need me." He stood up and walked out.

Inwardly, Emma groaned. Marcus would perceive this as an insult, and even though it was not of her making, he would place the blame at her door. As he often did. For now, her curiosity meant more than her concern at the reprisals.

"Excuse me, Mr Schilling, what can I do for you?" she asked.

The man looked at her, but he did not speak until Marcus closed the door behind him. He handed her a plain-looking business card, glossy white with text in blue.

"Schilling, Peterson, and Herring. Solicitors." She read from the card as though it would answer all her questions. "And?"

"Please, take a seat," he said, and gestured to one of the chairs in front of Marcus' desk. He smiled. "Forgive me, but I need to make sure you're who I think you are. You've been most difficult to locate, and we must not err. Not in this."

Emma frowned. "Am I difficult to find? I am in the phone book."

"I wish it were so simple. Still, we are here now. Might I be so bold as to ask a few questions first, before we get to the matter at hand?"

Emma nodded.

"You are Emma Blewitt?"

"Yes, I am she."

"Of flat three-B, number fourteen Church Row?"

"Yes."

"Daughter of Peter and Maureen Williams?"

"What? Oh no. That's not me. Not me at all." Her voice faltered.

"What?" Even Mr Cool and Contained looked a little flustered. Her answer had knocked his confidence. "Are you sure? Really sure?" He shook his head. "This is most irregular."

"Well, I think I should know who my…" Her voice faded away.

"Yes, yes, of course you would."

"I'm sorry, your question took me by surprise. You see, I was adopted as a small child. I was so young at the time that I've never known any family other than mom and dad. The ones who adopted me," she clarified.

"Of course, yes."

"It has been so long that I forget, sometimes, where I came from."

"Indeed. Forgive me, I made the assumption that your history would be known to you. Such an error is unforgivable."

As he spoke, he looked most contrite.

"No harm done. However, I do recall my biological parents were called Peter and Maureen. I never thought about my surname much. As I say, I was adopted so long that, as far as I am concerned, my name is Blewitt."

"I quite understand."

Memories filled her thoughts. "I remember. A long time ago, I saw the adoption papers." The details of her memory filled out and became more definite. In her mind's eye, she could see a pile of documents as though it sat on the desk in front of her. "Before the adoption, I was Emma Williams, daughter of Peter and Maureen Williams."

Emma watched as his shoulders eased, and he relaxed a little. "Good," he said, "You were so very young it is not surprising your birth name does not come immediately to mind. I should have accounted for that. No matter, we got there in the end."

"Perhaps. So, what's this all about?"

"We, that is the company, have been trying to locate you for quite a while. We were instructed by your aunt—"

"Aunt? What aunt?"

"Your aunt. More of a great aunt, I suppose. A Miss Maud Tapper of Castlecoombe."

"What? What are you talking about? I have no biological family. My parents looked. I looked."

"I appreciate that, but your mother—your birth mother—did have kin."

"No. Impossible. We looked." A hint of defensiveness crept into her tone. "There was no one. I'm sure."

"I think this is where I come in. Our researchers are second to none in most instances, and if something can be found, they will find it. You would have found your father, but Peter Williams has no surviving kin. I can confirm this to be true."

Emma nodded agreement.

"Your mother, Maureen, was Maureen Green before she got married. Her mother was Millicent Green. Am I correct so far?"

"Yes, Millicent Green, formerly Millicent Hardwick before she got married," Emma confirmed.

"Indeed, except it goes all wrong at this point."

"Excuse me?"

"Your grandmother, Millicent Green, or rather, Millicent Hardwick, does not exist."

"No, that can't be. I saw the records."

"I don't doubt that you did see the records, but were they the correct ones to show you the full truth?"

"I don't understand. I saw her birth certificate, the marriage certificate, and so on."

"This was a deception. The child born Millicent Hardwick died aged six months old and so could not have been married." Mr Schilling looked as distressed as Emma felt. "Let me explain. We believe your grandmother, one Millicent *Tapper*, worked for the National Archives."

"She worked for the government, then?"

"Yes, she dealt with collating records of births and deaths. That's where we think she found the records for the dead child, and she used those details to become someone else— Millicent Hardwick."

"You think? Do you not know for certain?"

"At this point, Miss Blewitt, we can only surmise what happened, and our guess is that, with some skillful doctoring of some key information, Millicent Tapper ceased to exist, and Millicent Hardwick took her place."

"This is too weird."

"Let me start at the beginning. Your grandmother Millicent Tapper of Castlecoombe, sister to Maud and Agnes Tapper, left home during the Second World War to help with the war effort. It was at this time that the family lost all trace of her. Our own investigations, tracked her to the National Archives, where we believe she was employed.

Emma didn't know what to say. "How long have you been looking into this?"

"Quite a few years."

"How many?"

"Six," he replied.

"Six years!"

"As you can appreciate, the records from that time are somewhat unreliable, and in times of such confusion it is easy for someone to disappear if they wish to. At this point, her trail seemed to vanish."

"She disappeared?"

"Well, yes. This was a regrettably common thing. Even if she hadn't changed her name, you have to realize it was a time of war. There was so much damage to places, to things, and to people. The world changed, records got lost, and people vanished. Back then, it was assumed, as so many families were forced to assume, she had perished in the bombing."

"But she didn't?"

"No. A few years later, she sent Maud a letter saying she was well, she was happy, and she had a child, but they would never see each other again. Maud let it pass. It was her belief Millicent would come back when she was ready."

"But she didn't, obviously."

"No, and although Maud accepted Millicent's choices, she missed her sister. One by one, her relations died, either from sickness or old age, and Maud thought it was time to restore what was left of the family. She instructed us to look for Millicent, or if the worst was discovered, for her descendants."

"What did you find?"

"We found you, of course, the last of the Tapper line. Unless you have children our searches have yet to discover?"

She shook her head. Words failed her, and even if she could have thought of something to say, the lump in her throat ensured she could not say it aloud. Her vision blurred, and she wiped away the tears at the corners of her eyes before they could fall. "So where do I find this great aunt? At Castlecoombe, is it?"

"I'm sorry, Miss Blewitt, but your aunt passed away some months ago."

Crushed hope almost brought Emma to her knees, and she stifled a sob. From his pocket, Mr Schilling produced a packet of tissues and offered her one. He waited until she had settled down before he continued. "It was her wish we should find you and pass on her legacy."

"I have a legacy?" She knew she sounded stupid, and her ability to form sentences left a lot to be desired, but she couldn't do anything about it. There was too much to process.

"Indeed you do."

Emma blew her nose.

"So," Mr Schilling continued, "I'm one of the primary executors of Maud Tapper's last will and testament, and it is a substantial holding. There will also be a refund of expenses, of course."

"A refund?"

"In the latter part of her life, Maud wanted us to spare no effort to find you, so our retainer was a substantial one." He blushed. "It was a straightforward commission until we started looking, and then it was clear Millicent didn't want to be found. Our efforts, I am saddened to say, were not as determined as they might have been. The unspent retainer will be refunded, which, in itself, amounts to a substantial sum."

"How did you find me?"

"Luck. One of the firm's partners is a historian who acquired a number of photographs from a newspaper covering some picnic event arranged by the war office. There he found a picture of Millicent Tapper holding the hand of a man later identified as Archie Green. It was our first and solitary lead, but it led to you. So it was all sheer luck."

"Oh."

"I understand this can be quite a lot to take in. Perhaps you should come to the office at your convenience, and we can get the required paperwork signed. I know we have discussed your identity, but I will require proof before we can finalize anything more. There is a lot to show you, and the sooner we attend to the details the sooner you can get your legacy."

"All right," she agreed.

"Now, take a few days if you like. If not, I will be at the address on the card I presented until quite late this evening."

Emma stared at the card for a few moments. "I'll be there," she promised. "I'll be there.

5

INHERITANCE

Emma sat at her desk and yawned so hard her face ached.

"What's up with you?" Barbara asked.

Emma put a finger to her lips. "Shush," she said. "Someone might hear."

Barbara gestured to the closed door that marked the edge of Marcus Riley's domain. "He's on a call, and he'll be too busy shouting at the telephone to notice what we're doing."

"Good."

Barbara smirked. "Come on then, spill. Who kept you up so late you're still yawning at this hour?"

"It's eight a.m."

"Just in time for lunch, then. What's her name and where did you meet?"

Emma laughed. "Get your mind out of the gutter."

"Gutter? Then you admit she kept you up all night. You whore!"

"I did no such thing."

"What a shame. You could do with someone keeping you up all night. Pity you wouldn't do anything so shameful, would you?"

"One day I'll shock you."

"I'll not hold my breath. So, if you haven't discovered new nocturnal habits, what's up, then?"

Emma glanced toward Marcus's office. "Can we talk about it later? We can grab a cup of coffee and chat."

"I have to wait?"

"Yes."

Barbara stared at her through narrowed eyes. "All right then, if you insist." She sighed dramatically. "I suppose I'll have to wait till lunch time. In that case, you can take me to The Royal Swan and buy me one of those bright blue drinks with the cherry and an umbrella."

Emma laughed.

Later, at The Royal Swan, Emma leaned against the counter and ordered two drinks, one of them bright blue with an umbrella, the other a tall glass of orange juice. She paid the server with cash and leaned back to face Barbara.

"So come on, spill," Barbara demanded.

"You know the guy who came in the other day? Looked like an undertaker?"

"I remember, yeah."

"He's a solicitor. My solicitor, it turns out."

"Since when have you had a solicitor?"

"Since long before I knew I did."

"Why? What have you done?" She sniggered. "Oh my god, you took a hit out on Marcus and the police found out."

Emma snickered. "Don't be silly."

"Okay, okay. Then why do you have a solicitor?"

"Because I have a family, Barbara, and they have been trying to find me."

"Oh my god!" Her face fell. "I thought they died. You went to the funeral. I went to the funeral with you."

"Not them, my biological family. The ones I tried to trace but never found."

Barbara nodded. "I thought…" She shook her head. "How do you feel about it?"

"I don't know. I was pleased at first, but it's too late to feel anything now. They're all dead."

"Emma, I'm so sorry."

Emma took a few moments to gather her thoughts. "It's okay. My feelings are so mixed at the moment. I'm sad because I lost them before I knew they existed. I'm sad, too, because I looked in all the wrong places and my efforts were wasted. At the same time, they're strangers to me, and I'm not sure if I feel anything toward any of them."

"It's a dilemma, I suppose."

"Yes," Emma agreed, "and it kept me awake last night."

"No wonder you look so tired. You must be distraught."

"I don't know them. I was so close, and now I've missed the one opportunity I ever had. I had an aunt, Barbara. A real aunt, related by biology and blood, and now she's dead. They're all dead, and I'm the last of a family I never knew I had."

"I'm sorry."

"Me too," Emma said.

"I know it must be hard to deal with this, but maybe you can find out more about them even though they're gone."

"Yes." She nodded as she sipped her orange juice. "There's more."

"More?"

"I'm rich. Well, as rich as someone like me can expect to be. My aunt has given me a house and some money. They've even made provision for any inheritance taxes to be paid, so what I get has already had the expensive costs deducted."

"So you're rich, huh? Rich enough I should dump my man and date you instead?"

Emma laughed in spite of herself. "No one is rich enough for you."

"True. I know you wanted to see them, to meet them, and

get to know them, but they're gone. I'm sorry, but at least you know they were there. Money, too. Life will be easier. You don't have to put up with a pig of a boss if you don't want to."

"I'd rather have a bunch of living and breathing relatives."

"I know, sweetie."

Emma smiled, but it was more of a grimace. "My house is in the country, you know, but I have no idea where it is, what it looks like, or anything. It could be a dump. What on earth will I do with a place in the country?"

"Sell it, love."

"I already have enough money. I have so much money I don't even need to work for a year or two at least. You know money doesn't mean anything. Not to me."

"Good God! You're going to quit your job."

"I've thought about it," Emma admitted. "But I'm not sure if I will or not. At least I have options now."

"Yes, you do, and about time you had a little luck."

"I think I'll go look at the house. My house. Maybe I can get a feel for them, for my ancestors. It sounds weird, but that's what they are."

"There you go. I knew you would soon see the positive side of things."

"If nothing else, I can see what I need to do to get the house sold on."

Barbara frowned. "There's something you're not telling me. I know you too well for you to hide things from me."

Emma didn't answer straight away. "Perhaps."

"You're chewing your lip. You only do that when you're uncertain or worried."

Emma laughed.

"Do you want to talk about it?"

"It's nothing."

"Nothing, you say?"

"Well, there's a feud, apparently."

"Go on."

"Yes, and this feud is hundreds of years old."

"That's so last century, but it sounds so interesting. Tell me more."

Emma took a small package from her bag and unwrapped a book no larger than her hand. It bulged with pieces of paper folded between the pages. "This is all the information I have about it."

"There's a feud, and someone kept records of it?"

"Well, not all of it. There is nothing here about how it started, which is a bit odd. If they kept records, why not record the story from the start? Still, it lists names and so on. I can pretty much trace my entire genealogical tree back hundreds of years and match it up with the other side of the family feud."

"It sounds odd, you know."

"I know. They have snippets of gossip written all over the place."

"Emma, your relations sound most bumpkinlike."

"Is there such a word?"

"Who cares?" Barbara answered. "It's all too country for me. I'm a city girl. I hardly know my neighbours, never mind would I hold a feud with them over generations."

"Me too, but I have to go and take a look."

"How long will you go for?"

"As long as it takes, I suppose. A few weeks perhaps? Maybe a little more."

"Has *he* agreed?"

"Has who agreed?"

"Marcus, of course. What has he said about all this?"

"Not told him yet."

"Interesting. I'd like to be there when you do. Can I watch?"

"You're a pervert, Barbara. And yes, you can watch if you want."

. . .

"You want to take how long off?" Marcus stormed.

"A month," Emma answered, and her voice was calmer than she felt. "Maybe more, but I think a month will do it."

"You're joking, aren't you?"

"No."

"What do you think I am, a bloody charity?"

"I don't expect to be paid whilst I'm gone."

"Too bloody right you're don't."

"I'd have thought you would be a little more understanding given the circumstances. It's been a tough year, and I haven't asked for much."

"Look, I know it's been hard losing your parents, and now you have a new aunt. But she's dead, Emma, and it's not like you knew her."

"That's not the point."

"The point is simple—I have a business to run."

"Yes, I'm aware of this, so I thought I'd wait until the end of the month. Plenty of time for me to finish my current projects. Then you can arrange a freelancer to cover my absence, and I can bring him or her up to speed before I go."

"End of the month? We'll be busy by then, I am sure. You know we always get busy at the end of the month."

Emma knew no such thing, but she would not give in. "Get the agency to send someone round as soon as they can, then."

"Do what you must."

"I will," Emma answered, and turned her attention back to her desk.

"I can't guarantee there will be work for you when you return. As I said, this isn't a charity."

Emma bit back her words. She didn't care what Marcus thought, she was going to Castlecoombe and that was that.

6

ON THE WAY

Darkness descended over the mountains with the speed and finality of a slammed door. Craggy peaks loomed large, and the dark– almost black – stone merged with the night. A light but persistent rain soaked everything under the sky and drummed the top of Emma's car, while the wipers cleared her windscreen with a steady and metronomic *whoosh*. The car headlamps picked out nearby features, but the sight of the cracked rock threatened more than reassured.

Emma drove through this unfamiliar landscape in a state of fear and apprehension. She didn't know the area; it wasn't a city, and if she looked too hard she could see all too many ways to crash. She clenched her teeth until her jaws ached and drove on.

If only she had left work at the time she'd planned to leave, then she would have reached Castlecoombe by now. If only Marcus hadn't been a complete tit and insisted she work until the evening rush hour had begun. Then she might have missed the worst of the weather, and perhaps reached her destination as the light started to fail.

Now that she thought about it, she couldn't say with any certainty why she'd needed to travel today. She should have taken the delay as an omen and stayed at home. A fresh start first thing in the morning would have been ideal. At least she wouldn't be driving through this godforsaken hole at the back of beyond.

Halfway through the mountains, the wind picked up. Sharp gusts blasted her little red city car from side to side. Distant flashes illuminated the peaks in stark bursts of bright light, and the afterglow lasted almost as long as the flash itself. A loud crack of thunder rocked the car, and Emma jumped in her seat.

"Shit!" she squealed.

The light rain, no more than a drizzle at first, soon became a torrential downpour. It speared the road with such ferocity it almost bounced into the sky again. Within minutes, the already saturated ground could hold no more. Water trickled between the rocks, gushed from every crevasse and turned the road into a fast-flowing river.

"Shit. Shit. Shit," she grumbled.

In these conditions, it was all too easy to lose sight of the road. She was halfway up a mountain, and she could see neither a pull-in nor a place to turn around, and no exits anywhere. She could only keep going.

Emma directed her gaze forward, gripped the steering wheel as though her life depended on it, and concentrated all of her attention on the road.

It would take one small lapse in concentration, a slip of the steering wheel, and she would fly over the edge and into the endless night. She slowed the car to little more than a crawl and peered through the windshield. Better slow than dead, she told herself.

Her fingers, pale and numb from her hold on the steering wheel, squeezed the wheel even tighter. On the passenger seat, her map mocked and enticed her to take one little peek. A quick look might tell her how far remained of her journey.

Then she would know how far she was from safety, and how much more of this she had to take.

She'd not seen a single vehicle in a long while. She could stop, take one small peek at the map. But with her luck, it might be the last thing she ever peeked at.

"Just drive," she told herself. "You got this."

At Ingerside, she found a collection of three houses and a pond nestled against the sheer sides of the Inger Peak. At least, she hoped it was the Inger. If it wasn't, she was lost.

Right then, she couldn't tell north from south, nor up from down. All of the roads looked the same, and there were not many roads to consider. None of the houses had lights on, so she couldn't stop anywhere and ask. She stopped beside the pond and looked at the map. She made some assumptions as to where she was, memorized the route, and restarted her journey. It would be easier now; it was all downhill. Yet that offered her no reassurance.

In the dark and the rain, the descent seemed too steep, the bends in the road too sharp and exposed. There were too many curves, the road slick with mud and leaves, and for one moment, Emma thought the car went sideways.

Then the road flattened out and in the darkness she saw the twinkling of lights. She made out a small sign by the side of the road. She had arrived.

In the darkness, the village of Castlecoombe hunkered down against the driving rain to merge, almost unseen, with the soaring granite peaks. To Emma, whose architectural preferences ran towards steel, glass, and hundreds of lights, this was a vista from hell. She had expected a small town, but what she saw wasn't even big enough to be a village, never mind a town. There weren't any streetlights, and without their reassuring glow, the place looked derelict. If it hadn't been for a few spots of muted light that spilled from different buildings, she would have thought the place abandoned.

Emma sighed. The country seemed a dark, miserable,

cold, and wet place to be. She couldn't escape the thought that coming here had been a terrible mistake.

She headed towards the lights and found herself at a place where the road looped around a small green no larger than the twisted tree at its center. She stopped at the side of the road and spared a quick glance at her map and the hastily drawn sketch and instructions she'd been given.

The road, as expected, turned full circle and left the way it came in. A single road turned off onto a narrow street, and at the farthest point of the circle, a grand and turreted gatehouse marked the driveway to Magwood Hall. All as expected.

It's the Addams Family's winter retreat, she thought, and the so-called bane of her entire line. She wondered what such people would be like.

She shook her head at the way her thoughts went. At least she had survived the drive through the mountains. She thought of home, the city, and the stories she would be able to tell Barbara.

Emma checked her mirrors, even though she hadn't seen another car in a long while, and pulled back onto the road. She drove around the loop, past the gate house entrance, and back on herself, as though she were about to drive straight back out of the village. There she stopped and turned the key to kill the engine.

The house she sought was more modest than the gatehouse and stood in the middle of a short terrace of six cottages. The numbers on the doors were hard to see in the dark and the rain, but she counted along the front doors and stopped outside the one fronted by a profusion of weeds. This had to be the one. Without lights of any kind, shadows shrouded the whole row of houses. Hers, though, had an air of darkness so deep it was like looking into the depths of a deep well.

Small and unkempt she could deal with, but this dingy

place looked several steps beyond that. It was so unappealing that Emma wanted to turn around and leave.

She stared through her car windows at the few houses she could see. Darkness and rain made her observations more difficult.

She leaned back in her seat and closed her eyes. Her mind drifted, and when she thought about the rain, the sound made her think of a hundred feet running over the car roof, every one of them in a rush to escape Castlecoombe. She thought about Barbara, who had advised her to get someone to do everything for her. There were companies who would empty Maud's house, renovate it, and sell it on. That idea appealed more than she would have admitted at the time.

She couldn't do it, though. She had such a need to get a sense of who she was and where she had come from. But that need brought with it a whole world of guilt. Her parents, the couple who had adopted her, had been fabulous, loving parents and she'd loved them.

Why am I here?

The guilt rose up and sat like a stone gargoyle hunched upon her shoulders. How could she even think to replace her parents? Is that what I'm doing? she wondered. In her mind's eye, she could see them as clearly as they had been in life.

Yet, no matter how much she thought of them, there remained a hole where her biological family should have been. Her need to know was such a commanding imperative she could never turn away from the opportunity to learn more.

She opened her eyes and stared at the rundown house. The hole they left could not, would not, be filled, no matter what she did.

"Right then, Maud. Let's see what you have to say for yourself," she said. It was time to find out who she was, and, with luck, why her biological grandmother had felt the need to hide.

Emma bent over the passenger seat so she could access the glove box. Inside, she rummaged around until she grabbed a small torch and the front door key. It was a big old-fashioned chunky affair, straight out of a museum. This simple lump of metal did not inspire confidence in security.

She gripped her thin and inadequate jacket around her body and got out into the rain. She raced to the front door and the slight overhang her solicitor had – with an amount of optimism bordering on comedic – called a storm porch. Rain dripped over her collar, and she shivered as drops of cold water ran down her neck. In her hand, the key glinted in the wavering torch light, and doubt stayed her hand. This was her last chance, the point of no return. Once she opened the door, there would be no going back.

Beyond the dark and uninviting front door lay a past in which she had no part. Her heart ached with lives, lost lives, and a family she did not and could not know. Inside would be like a mausoleum to the dead. She shivered. The place already gave her the creeps, which added to her own misgivings.

She stared at the door, and it looked all wrong. Her torch, "SUPABRITE – perfect illumination," turned out to offer no more than an insipid pool of yellow, with barely enough power to light the lock, never mind anything else. There had to be something not right about a place so dark it seemed to devour light instead of embrace it.

Movement, a pale flash of something, caught her eye.

"Damn!" She jumped back, but when she shone her weak torch into the darkness, she saw nothing. Bloody shadows.

She placed the oversized key in the lock and turned it. The loud *ker-clunk* of the mechanism echoed behind the solid wood, and although she knew the door was unlocked, she didn't rush to open it. The door handle, another ancient piece of brass work, looked huge and menacing in its own right. When she used the handle, it turned with a solid but smooth motion. Not so much the hinges, though, and with a yawning screech the front door creaked open.

The musty aroma of age, dampness, and disuse gushed out. Emma wrinkled her nose; she would need to leave a few windows open for sure. She shone her torch into the narrow hall, and it illuminated vague piles of letters and newspapers on the floor. She ignored the mail; it had waited this long; it could wait a little longer. The more important search for the light switch took a moment. She flicked it up and down several times, but nothing happened.

"Dammit!" she cursed. She maneuvered her way through the hall to the first doorway to find another light switch. When the second switch didn't work, she cursed a little more. It seemed the world was conspiring against her.

Perhaps it was time to return to civilization and find a hotel. She did not fancy the trip through the mountains, but there had to be a town, anywhere else. She turned to leave.

A scream froze on her lips when she found herself staring along the length of twin barrels pointed at her chest. Emma stood statue-still, unable to look anywhere other than at the gun.

"Who the hell are you?" a deep, female voice demanded.

Her torch, all but forgotten, pointed at the floor. A pale yellow glow, it illuminated nothing. It didn't even occur to Emma to lift the beam and get a better look at the figure before her.

"Did you hear me?" the woman asked.

Emma tore her eyes from the weapon. It wasn't the first gun she had ever seen and, living in the city, it wouldn't be the last. Her gaze floated upward to look at the shadow woman. Framed by the doorway, she was tall, but not to the point of being lanky. She was slim, too, despite the bulk of the full-length overcoat that broadened her shoulders. A practical, but unattractive, wide-brimmed hat covered her head and cast her face deeper in shadow. Rain collected on the brim and splashed from there to her shoulders and from there onto the stone floor and some of the old newspapers Emma had failed to pick up. If anything, the woman looked like some wild, angry beast come to show her what the country had to offer.

Emma had met some scary characters on her doorstep before, and she wasn't going to allow some wild country woman to see how scared she was. Instead, she drew back her shoulders and affected her best deadeye stare.

"And who the hell are you?" she growled. She tried to put as much menace as she could muster into the words, in spite of the fact she held nothing more intimidating than a plastic torch. "Threatening me in my own house!"

"*Your* house, you say?" the woman asked. Her apparent aggression wavered. "This is your house?"

"Yeah, this is my house." She bristled with as much indignation as she could manage. "So point your weapon elsewhere, or I'll have you arrested." She didn't ask if they even had a police force in these parts.

The barrels of the shotgun dipped a little further and then pointed at the floor. The woman had the cheek to laugh. "Mrs. Blewitt? Mrs. Emma Blewitt? Goodness, you have a temper."

"Miss Blewitt, thank you." She took a step forward to press her advantage, and when she remembered her torch, shone the feeble light into the woman's face. She noticed then the bright shining blue eyes and ready smile. "And you are?"

The woman seemed unsure for a moment. "Maggie," she answered.

"Maggie?"

"I'm so rude," she mumbled. She removed her hat and ran her fingers through her hair. She stuck out her hand. "I'm Maggie Durrant. I live at the Hall up on the hill. When I saw lights bobbing about the place, I thought you were a burglar."

Emma didn't answer at first; she was too busy taking it all

in. Maggie was not what she'd expected. She'd thought to find an old fuddy-duddy chap with a mean eye and a nasty hatred of all things Tapper, and therefore Blewitt. Instead, Maggie was a young woman—probably not much different from Emma herself. Her blue eyes twinkled now that her face was no longer hidden in the shadow of her hat, and she didn't look as mean as Emma had imagined either.

She grasped the proffered hand before the woman had a chance to change her mind. In this place at the back of nowhere, she needed all the help she could get.

"Are you the Lord Durrant?" she asked.

"Indeed, I am. You've heard of me?"

"Well, yes. But how many burglars use a key and park their car outside the door?"

"Well… I didn't see how you got in. I saw the lights."

"But you knew who I was."

"If you have a key, then you could be only one person, the relative of Maud Tapper. I had a letter from a solicitor to say they had discovered to whom the house now belonged and to expect you at some point."

"So do I call you Lady Durrant? Or is it Lord? I've not met a lord before."

The woman laughed, and it was a loud and cheerful laugh. The humor echoed through the empty house until the building felt less sad than it had. "Only if you hate me, but given the way I introduced myself at the end of a shotgun, perhaps you already do. Anyway, I would prefer Maggie."

"Does everyone call you Maggie?" Emma asked, gesturing in such a way as to include the whole village.

Maggie shook her head. "To them I am the Lord Durrant. It keeps them happy to know someone is responsible."

"Responsible? For what?"

"For everything," Maggie answered. "Someone has to be responsible."

"I'm not sure I understand what you mean."

"I'm not sure I do sometimes, either." Maggie shrugged. "You'll get to know the way things work the longer you're here."

Emma nodded, but her mind whirled. With Maggie stood before her, all of the information she'd received seemed insufficient. She'd stumbled on a puzzle, but the clues had been so jumbled, they had become distant and fantastical. The best she could do, the best thing to do, was change the subject. "Blasted electrics are off, and the utility company promised they'd reconnect by today."

"They did reconnect," Maggie answered. "Telephones, too."

"But I have no lights."

"With the storm, we lost power three or four hours ago. It'll be like this until the weather clears and someone can get out to fix stuff."

"If it ever stops."

"Indeed."

"But I can see lights in the other houses."

"That's because they have generators. Even when we don't have bad weather, the supply of power can be a little temperamental, so wherever possible residents get generators. If not, they learn to make do with candles and torches."

Emma almost didn't dare ask. "Do I have one?"

"I would expect you do, yes." Maggie looked at the woman in front of her. "I see you are not attired for the country, are you?"

"Well, no," Emma admitted. "I'm a city girl. Is it that obvious?"

Maggie grinned. "Do you want me to look around the back and fire it up for you?"

Emma nodded. "Would you? It's kind of you to be so helpful. I'm cold, I'm tired, I'm hungry and thirsty, and if something doesn't change soon, I think I'll curl up in the corner and scream. Unless there is a proper coffee shop nearby with at least half a dozen different types of coffee and several ways to serve hot chocolate?"

Maggie laughed a deep throaty chuckle, and Emma smiled in spite of everything. "Funny. Do you think Castlecoombe is the kind of place to have a coffee house?" She shook her head. "I better get the generator started, then." Maggie rested her gun against the back of the door and took a Maglite from her coat pocket. When she tested the light, the bright white beam was powerful enough to illuminate both women. Maggie froze.

"Are you all right? You look like you've seen a ghost," Emma said.

"Yes. I think I have." Maggie answered.

She watched the smile dawn on Maggie's face, but it looked stiff and forced, not at all the cheery grin she'd given earlier.

"I'm sorry, I'll go and fix the generator," she said, and she strode through the house as though she knew it well.

7

POWER UP

Maggie couldn't wait to be outside, even in the bad weather. She leaned against the wall and stared into the rain. She closed her eyes as cold drops splashed onto her face and chilled her straight through.

It was her.

Her knees threatened to give way, and she was not at all sure how she'd managed to make it this far.

Her. Her Tapper.

The woman from her dreams, enticing her with those dark brown Tapper eyes. The face in her dreams stared at her with that unrelenting gaze, but in person she seemed so different. Her dreams could never match the woman she had just met, and when Emma smiled, she was nothing like all the dour Tappers Maggie had seen.

She wiped her face. She couldn't stand here all night. Her bright beam flashed around the small backyard to two outbuildings, one of which probably housed the generator. The first one contained rusty garden implements and a few logs. Inside the second, she found what she sought. She fiddled with the engine, checked the hoses, primed it, and switched it on.

Thank goodness Maud had installed a decent machine and not one of the old-style generators with the pull cord. She'd have been outside all night trying to get the engine to catch. She flicked the gauge a few times, but this baby wasn't going to run for long, not unless it was so efficient it could run on fumes.

She didn't go back straight away. Now that she had completed her mission to provide power, her thoughts could race wherever they wished. She'd wanted to hate the Tapper heir, but she couldn't. How could she, when she had stared at this dream woman most nights for years?

P ower returned to the house with a flicker and a hiss that threatened to vanish as soon as it arrived. A few lights flickered, and then held steady.

"Yes!" Emma cried, and punched the air in victory. Yet her victory was short lived. Half the lights remained dark, and those that worked, of the old incandescent sort, offered such dim illumination that they weren't much help. Then again, dim light was better than none at all.

Maggie came back into the house, put her hat to the side, and shrugged out of her coat. "I'm sorry about dripping all over your floor."

Emma waved her off. "It's a small price to pay to get lights. Thank you for doing that for me."

"You're very welcome."

Emma turned to look down the dark hallway. "It's still so dark in here. Better than nothing, though, I suppose." She shrugged. "I'll put the kettle on, if it works."

"That would be lovely. I don't think you will be doing much more tonight. Your fuel tank is almost empty. Also, I took a look at your gas tank. That's almost empty, too, so there's no gas for the cooker and limited electricity."

"Damn. Well, that buggers up my plans for the evening already."

"You had plans for tonight?"

"Yes. I'd hoped to get started on sorting things out."

"You don't like to waste time, then."

"No, I don't," Emma said. The kettle reached a boil. "It's time for tea." She searched through the cupboards and drawers until she found all she needed. "Do you think this packet of loose tea is safe to drink?"

"If it's dry, yes," Maggie answered.

Emma opened the antique electrical refrigerator in the corner of the room. She took one look and wrinkled her nose. "There is nothing useful here. I hope you like black tea. I've milk somewhere in the back of my car, but I don't fancy unloading anything right now."

"Black is fine."

"Good. And don't blame me if this tea is vile."

"Hot and wet is fine on a night like this."

Once done, Emma placed two mugs filled with hot tea on the small kitchen table. She took a seat as though she'd always sat here and gestured to one of the seats. "Make yourself comfortable."

Maggie folded herself with grace and elegance into a seat and sat with her back straight, her posture stiff and formal.

"You can relax and make yourself comfortable."

"I am comfortable, thank you," Maggie answered. She sipped at her over hot tea and winced. "Whew, that's a potent brew. Do you mind if I help myself to a little sugar? If you have some?"

"Help yourself," Emma said, and pointed at the ceramic sugar bowl. "Looks safe."

Maggie leaned over to get the bowl of sugar. A box of cereal fell from the top shelf, and if she hadn't leaned to one side, it would have landed square on the top of her head.

Emma looked confused. "I'm sorry. I must have knocked the cabinet or something."

Maggie waved her off. "It's okay, I'm used to it."

"What? Used to being assaulted by cereal boxes?"

Maggie laughed. "Something like that, yes."

"I hope nothing else in the house assaults you whilst you are here as my guest."

"Does that apply to uninvited guests like myself?"

"Yes, so long as you leave the gun outside."

Maggie sipped at her tea. "What do you plan to do? Now you're here?"

"In principle? Or tonight specifically?" She paused as though to gauge Maggie's answer, and then continued. "Well, in principle, I'm not sure. Tonight, I'd hoped to get a good start on sorting things out. Well, maybe not sorting everything out, not in one night, at least. I need to get a feel for things to see what needs fixing, what needs to be thrown away, and what I can use. That sort of thing. Now I'm here, the light levels are not helpful, it's freezing, and I can't find the central heating boiler."

"You won't find a boiler here. If you want warmth, then you need to make a fire in the fireplace. If this is like the other houses on this row, then the fire will also act as your water heater, too."

"No heating!"

"Central heating has appeared at some of the larger and newer houses, but we're all used to logs and coal. When you live out here, you get to rely on things that have survived the test of time. Things don't change much in the country, you see. At least not with any great speed."

Emma groaned. "No central heating. This is more basic than I could have imagined. I think I need more than tea. I need something with wine or brandy in it. I suppose it'll be like camping out, but inside a house. It'll be an adventure."

"You're not from around these parts, are you?"

"Is it so obvious?"

"Yes. Apart from the accent, well, you look like you're dressed for a meeting, not a drive through the country. Heels instead of boots, and your clothing is far too thin for this weather. You'll catch your death of cold. Do you have thicker clothes, or a thick sweater at least?"

"In my suitcase. I'm sure I might have a fleece or two, but I didn't pack for this weather."

Maggie looked thoughtful. "You look damp and uncomfortable. I wonder—"

Emma waited for Maggie to continue, and when she didn't, she prompted her. "What did you wonder, Lord Durrant?"

"Maggie," she corrected.

"All right, then. What did you wonder?"

"Well, I did wonder, seeing as you're a city girl, whether you intend to stay here or whether this is a quick look at your Castlecoombe assets?"

"Ahh. As to that, I could say it's none of your business." She smiled to take the sting out of her words. "But my real answer would be a simple 'I don't know.'"

"I see," Maggie said as she sipped her tea.

"Do you country folk always look at people and judge them on what you see?"

Maggie shrugged. "We're simple people."

Emma stared at her. "Simple?"

"Yes. If the little red thing outside is yours, it's not an ideal vehicle for driving over the mountains in foul weather like this. And someone who drives such a car is not going to be staying long."

"Sounds a fair assumption," Emma agreed. "I didn't intend to arrive so late. I work in the city. Well, I do now, but my boss played awkward about this trip. To be honest, I'm not even sure I have a job any more, but I'll cross the employment bridge when I need to." She sighed.

"Sometimes I wish I could tell my boss what to do with his job."

"Maybe you should. There's no need to spend your working life with an unpleasant boss who's being horrible."

"True enough, I suppose. Anyway, I could have waited until morning to come, but I had to leave the moment I had a chance. I'm not sure why, but I needed to get here fast."

"Or get away?"

Emma chuckled to herself. "Maybe there was an element of that as well."

"Did you know your aunt well?"

Emma stared through the doorway into the dim lounge. "Actually, I never knew I had an aunt until a few weeks ago. So everything is strange and new. Including this house, and a family I never knew I had."

"That sounds like a story and a half. Maybe you'll share it over a bottle of wine or something."

"That would be lovely. You're very kind."

"It's no more than anyone else would do."

Emma shook her head. "Not at all. I live in the city, and helping anyone is not really a part of the culture there."

"In that case, I will try to make you as welcome as I can."

"Thank you. I appreciate your help. For a start, I'd never have worked out how to get the power on all by myself."

"My pleasure. And what do you think now? I know this is not the best time to judge things."

"Interesting, I think. There is a lot to take in, but I really needed to know what was here," Emma answered.

"Maybe you'll like it and decide to stay."

"Early days yet." Emma's gaze flicked over the small kitchen and the dated fittings and appliances. She wondered whether this was the kind of place she wanted to live.

"It's a small house, I know, but most people are very comfortable in the same houses around here," Maggie said.

"It's still larger than my flat."

"Really?"

"But it's not in the city," Emma said. She thought it looked depressing, too, but she didn't want to say that out aloud.

Maggie nodded. "It would make sense to keep your options open, then."

Emma sighed. "I'm not sure sense has anything to do with this."

"Oh?" Maggie pulled herself upright, as though on alert.

"To cut a long story short, I think I need to know where I come from. It sounds silly, I suppose, but it means something to me."

"It's not silly at all. It's important, I think, to know your heritage."

"Thank you."

"You know, you look so much like Maud, it's uncanny."

"I do?"

Now Maggie stared at her intently. "Yes, you do."

"How well did you—" Emma jumped from her seat. "What the hell!"

"Emma? What's the matter?" Maggie jumped from her seat and moved to Emma's side.

Emma flinched as a gust of wind rattled the window. "There's someone outside."

"What? In this weather?"

"You were outside in this weather. A bit of rain didn't stop you."

"I didn't say I was normal, though, did I?"

"No, you didn't."

They stared at each other for a moment.

"What did you see?" Maggie asked.

"White," Emma said. "I saw white."

Maggie pulled on her hat, grabbed her coat, and stood by the door, ready to go outside. She flicked on her torch. "I'll look." She opened the door and stepped into the rain.

"She was white," Emma said.

Maggie had already left, and the door thudded closed behind her.

Emma shivered. Without Maggie in the room, it seemed colder, darker, and even more sinister. She wrapped her arms around her waist and almost jumped out of her skin when Maggie came back through the door.

"No one there," she declared as she removed her wet things.

"You sound rather cheerful considering you've just been out in the cold rain again."

Maggie waved a white plastic bag in the air. "This was stuck on a bush. Perhaps it blew by the window as you looked out."

"I don't think so."

"You know, in this weather, things look strange and odd." She placed the sodden bag into the rubbish.

"It wasn't a bag I saw," Emma insisted. "It was a someone."

"It was an illusion, Emma. Nothing more."

"I saw her. She was all white, with dark hair."

Maggie looked sympathetic, but Emma knew she didn't believe her.

"Never mind. No matter what you think, I know what I saw," Emma said. Anger rose up and her fear receded. She would never forget the image of the woman in the window. The dirty white clothes, the pale face, and the dark, desolate eyes staring through the kitchen window.

She shivered. The face, the anguish in those eyes, would haunt her always, and the thought of being alone in the house tonight, without anyone, did not appeal.

"You're cold. Do you have anything warmer to wear?"

"Car," Emma answered.

"We'll get something in a moment. But we should look around the rest of the house. Make sure it's all safe and so on," Maggie suggested. "We can get a feel for the place, plan what needs to be done before it gets too cold, and before the generator runs out of fuel."

Emma nodded. "It's very kind of you to be so helpful, but don't you have your own things to do? I don't want to suck up all your time." She sounded so polite, but the last thing she wanted was for Maggie to go and leave her alone.

"Nothing to do on a night like this, and there's no one but my brother and I at the house. If anything, I welcome the distraction."

"Well, as long as you don't mind."

"I don't mind at all. Truth be told, I'm a little nosey."

"Lord of some posh hall and you want to see the insides of my aunt's house?"

"Yes," she answered, unruffled. "I told you I was nosey."

"Good, then I think I'll be able to pump you for information about my aunt and the rest of the family."

Maggie shrugged. "Maybe later, but for now, shall we make a start and look around your house?"

"My house," Emma repeated.

"Yes?"

"My house. One I own. Which means I'm finally solvent. Well, kinda."

"Good for you." Maggie grinned.

"But this house gives me the creeps."

"Does it?" Maggie asked.

"Don't you think so?"

Maggie shook her head. "Not at all. Why is that?"

"It's too quiet, too rural." As soon as the words were out of her mouth, she reconsidered what she meant. "It's too noisy."

"Which one did you mean? Too noisy or too quiet?"

"Both. I live with the sounds of perpetual traffic, trains from the local subway, slamming doors, and loud music. Those are the sounds of people living in close proximity, and they're always there."

"It sounds dreadful."

"Not after you get used to it. It fades into the background, so you know it's there, but it's of no concern any more. This quiet is very loud and disturbing."

"You do know that doesn't make sense."

"Listen to the rain. Like a snare drum." She cocked her head to one side. "And there's the wind. It howls and growls as it comes closer and goes further away. Trees and hedges shake in the wind and rain and rattle against the windows. Even the house makes noises. The creaks and groans never stop. Like it's talking some language *it* understands and no one else does."

"Now you make it sound really ominous."

"It is! Nothing is normal here. Outside, the dark is so deep and complete that even shadows hide. I know they're there, though, and they are hiding. Waiting for me, even."

Maggie shuddered. "Now you're giving me the creeps."

"Good." Emma nodded with some satisfaction. "I'm glad it's not just me, then."

Maggie laughed and grabbed Emma's hand. "Come on, let's look around the house. I'm right here, so the shadows won't swallow you."

"Thanks. If I wasn't jittery before, I am now."

At the top of the stairs, Maggie paused. Emma watched steam jet from her mouth as she spoke. "You know, I expected the house would be chilly, but upstairs it's much worse. The cold is bitter and inhospitable. You can't stay here, not until it is made more habitable. Perhaps you ought to come over to the Hall, where it's warmer."

"Seriously, you're inviting me to stay at the Hall?"

Maggie nodded. "I'd be happier to know you're safe, rather than here where it's not. As I said, it's not ready for habitation."

"If it's no bother?" She was not going to get many opportunities like this.

"No bother at all. I assume you're not some psycho with a chainsaw?"

Emma laughed.

"Well? Are you?" Maggie prompted.

"The chainsaw's in the car."

Maggie snorted as she grabbed her gun. "Come on, then. Let's go."

Emma borrowed her aunt's old overcoat. It had seen better days and smelled damp and musty, but when she wrapped it around her shoulders, she had to admit it was warmer than anything she owned. It would keep the worst of the rain from her shoulders, and Emma would be thankful for such mercies.

"We can take my car," Emma yelled over the rain and wind. "I'm not walking anywhere."

"I know." Maggie pointed at Emma's feet. "I've seen your shoes, and trust me, they won't last two minutes here."

Emma looked at her feet. "They're good shoes."

"If you're going to a ballroom dance, yes. Here, you'll break your ankles."

Emma lifted her toes and rested on the heels of her feet. "They're comfortable, though, and it's not like I'm wearing high heels. What do you suggest I wear?"

"Wellies," Maggie said.

8

DRIVE

Maggie folded herself into Emma's tiny car and hunched over her knees so she wouldn't put her head through the roof. She didn't consider herself to be overly tall, but this car exaggerated her height to the point that she thought it more suitable for hobbits than humans.

"Small and dinky, isn't it? Bet you can park it anywhere," she said.

"I can, yes."

"More room in a wheelbarrow though," she observed.

"Yes, but unlike a wheelbarrow, this has a roof," Emma replied. "It's not even the smallest of cars either."

"There are cars smaller than this one? Seriously?"

"Very seriously."

"I don't understand that. I'm not tall, and I have trouble getting in this one, never mind anything smaller."

"Well, if it's too tight for you, I could always chop your head off, then you'd fit without a problem."

Maggie chuckled. "But you left the axe in the back, and you don't want to go out into the rain."

"It needs to be sharpened before I use it anyway."

"I'm not sure this car is big enough for a full-sized axe. Are you sure there aren't hobbits in your family tree?"

Emma stared at her. "For all I know there are hobbits and dragons in my family."

"I'm sorry, that was insensitive of me."

Emma grunted, started the engine, and pulled away from the curb. "Hold on," she warned.

"Why?" Yet Maggie grabbed the handhold and held on as Emma threw the little car around the green and swung around by the gatehouse.

"What a gorgeous building. Shame it's fallen to ruin." Emma slowed the car to crawling speed, and they inched under the arched gateway. Two towers, several floors high, soared into the night. Numerous flying buttresses, elegant and ornate, looked like giant spiders climbing each tower.

To Maggie, it looked different this dark night, but that may have had something to do with being curled up and closer to ground level.

"It's a fascinating example of mock gothic architecture. You wait until you see the house."

"I bet it's really grand, isn't it?"

Maggie shrugged. "You might want to keep the speed down on the way up. The road is narrow and steep. With this rain, it will be quite slippery, too."

Emma kept her speed down as instructed. "It's a fair way. I wonder how you saw me arrive from way up here."

"I didn't say I was at the house."

"Where were you?"

"I was in the gatehouse. At the top of the west tower, in fact. I often stand up there."

"On a night like this, why would you be at a ruin?"

Maggie paused to look out the window. "It's where I wait."

"Wait? What on Earth for?"

"For you."

Emma slammed on the brakes, and the wheels slipped on the sodden and wet road.

Maggie, already in an awkward and uncomfortable position, gripped the dashboard and hoped for the best. "Dammit, Emma, you almost drove off the road."

Emma turned to face Maggie. "Excuse me. What did you say?"

Maggie looked at Emma's face. Even in the dim interior of the car, her eyes were wide. She looked stunned, or scared, Maggie wasn't entirely sure which. The sound of rain drumming on the roof filled the car whilst she thought of what to say.

"What did you mean?" Emma repeated. "Why would you wait for me? That sounds crazy, you know."

"I knew you would come. I had to wait for you."

"Maggie, you're weirding me out here."

"I can explain. I promise."

"So, it turns out you are some axe-wielding homicidal lord, then."

Maggie laughed, but there was not the slightest hint of humor in the sound. "Far from it." Her laugh turned into a grimace. "I'll wager you'll be the death of me."

"Maggie…"

"Let's go to the house, shall we? Better to be in some comfort for this conversation."

Emma seemed to pause for a moment, then she put the car into gear and resumed her drive.

9
—————

THE HALL

I f Emma thought the gatehouse looked impressive, the hall overwhelmed her.

"Well," Maggie mumbled, "here we are. Welcome to the old pile."

"This? This is Magwood Hall?"

"Indeed."

"Hall? This is not a hall. It's a huge castle!"

"Oh no, it's not a castle. In fact, in the beginning, it was quite modest, a farmstead manor, but it grew. Then they fortified with a license to crenellate, and it all went from there, really. Each generation added something more to the mix. Perhaps they wanted to make their mark, but my forebears grew more extravagant with each generation."

"I should think they did." Emma stared at the hall, and even with the poor visibility through a mountain storm, it was a commanding edifice. Towers with witch-hat turrets and even more flying buttresses. "Extravagant ancestors? Is that what you call it?"

Maggie shrugged. "Yeah, one or two of them got a little showy, I think." She pointed into the rain. "If you drive through those gates, we can unload in the courtyard."

"You have a courtyard?"

"Yes, it's on the other side of the wall. The gates lead into a tunnel that goes through the outer wall."

"An outer wall means there is an inner wall."

Maggie laughed. "Just the one wall. We call the inside edge the inner wall, to avoid confusion."

"Right," Emma said.

She drove through the gates, into the tunnel, and through the wall. It turned out that the wall was about fifty feet thick in this section. "Is it all like this?"

"Where the walls still exist, yes."

"It would be a formidable defensive structure," Emma observed.

"Yes. I'll show you one day, when it's daylight and not raining so much."

"I'd like that," Emma replied.

Beyond the wall, the car headlamps picked out the main features of the gravel-covered courtyard. The hall to one side, the walls extending beyond the range of the headlamps, and a couple of outbuildings on the far side that could easily be a dozen houses.

"Goodness, it's huge," Emma said.

"Park right next to the main doors, over there." Maggie pointed in the direction she meant. "I usually use the back door, but when it rains like this, the front door is covered enough for me to avoid getting too wet."

At almost the same time, they jumped out of the car and raced for the small portico that covered the front door. Dim light spilled across the double doors and the ground in front. Maggie removed a chunky Chubb key from her coat pocket and slid it into the lock.

Emma grabbed a small suitcase and a small gym bag from the boot of the car and raced up the few steps of the portico into shelter.

"Let me help you," Maggie said. She took one of the bags from Emma and pushed the door open. "This way."

Emma wasn't really listening. There was too much to look at. A tiny vaulted antechamber offered a place to wipe her feet and opened into a huge vaulted entry hall. Arched doors stood to the left and right, and fluted marble columns stretched up to the ceiling vaults. To the side, a wide stone staircase with carved uprights and covered with ornate decoration led upward.

"Like it?" Maggie asked.

"This is very impressive."

Maggie shrugged. "It's just a house."

Emma thought about her tiny flat. The whole thing would fit into this hallway and she could park the car next to it without touching the walls. "Yeah, it's just a house and nothing more. I can see that."

Maggie turned to face her and frowned. "I'm merely a caretaker of the building and the land." She shrugged. "We can take your bags upstairs now, if you like, and then I'll make some tea. I have milk, too."

"Sounds great."

"Come on, this way." Maggie bounced up the stairs with Emma's bag in one hand. "The east wing is where we'll stay. West wing used to be for guests, but we don't use it now. Well," she paused as though thinking of the words to use, "I don't use it. My brother has decided to commandeer that end of the building for himself."

"So you have a wing each, then."

"Yes." Maggie walked away and opened one of the doors. "Here we are. You can stay here, if you like."

The room was substantia, and contained a standard double bed, a walnut wardrobe, and a matching dressing table. A couple of armchairs and a small side table to one side made the place look cozy even though the lights didn't work.

"Of course, there are no lights here at the moment, and

candles are all we have. I'll find you a storm lantern later, but not until you've warmed yourself up by the fire."

"This is lovely," Emma said.

"It's a bit dusty."

"No, it's nice. I like it."

"Thank you. It's kind of you to say, but we don't get many guests, so it's not a high priority on the maintenance agenda. I don't have many staff on duty anymore." She shrugged. "It is what it is."

"And it is delightful."

"Would you like to settle in first, or would you prefer to come downstairs?"

"I'm sure I'll get lost if you leave me alone. I'd rather follow you down."

Maggie looked pleased at her response. "Your comfort and security are my number one priority. I will not leave you unattended at any point."

"Even when I go to sleep?"

Maggie opened her mouth, then closed it again. Whatever she had intended to say got lost somewhere between brain and mouth.

"I'm teasing. It's a bad habit," Emma said.

"Do you tease everyone you meet?"

"Only the cute ones," she answered.

Maggie muttered something to herself and led the way downstairs.

Emma shook her head. This wasn't like her at all. Her stomach churned and a wave of cold rushed through her whole body. She recognized the sensation as nervous anxiety. A pity she couldn't keep her mouth shut when her nervousness switched her brain off.

In as much as Emma could see in the dim half-light provided by the few working lamps, the parts of the hall they passed through could only be described as grand. Even the shadows couldn't hide all the vaulted archways, ceilings, great pillars, pilasters, and other great architectural features. Big and imposing, ornate to the point of ostentatious, the whole building glorified the skills of artisans long gone. There was nothing ordinary or contemporary about this residence, even the cobwebs were complex silvery designs.

The vast grandness overwhelmed Emma, and not for the first time since she'd arrived at Castlecoombe, she wondered what the hell she was doing here. When something caught her eye, a carved section or a painting, she wanted to stop and stare, to put it all into some kind of perspective. But Maggie strode on and didn't stop until they reached the main hall.

Which was thirty feet or so wide, and at least double that in length.

Maggie stood next to a fireplace almost as tall as she was. She prodded at the fire in the grate and threw on a couple of logs. Emma wondered if she could park her car in that fireplace.

"Like it?" Maggie asked.

"What?" Emma replied, surprised by the question.

"Do you like it?"

"This whole house is stunning. It's like something from television."

"But do you like it?"

"It's very impressive," she said. Emma stared at the fire and refused to be overwhelmed by it all.

"I guess so. Anyway, are you hungry? Can I get you anything to eat? Tea? Coffee?"

"I'm starving. I stopped at a service station on the way, but the food there was not the most appetizing." She smiled. "But please, I don't want to be any bother."

Maggie beamed. "No bother at all. Come, come. Let's see what we have in the kitchen."

If asked, Emma didn't think she would ever recall the way from the hall to the kitchen. To her mind, they'd walked several miles and changed direction so many times she wouldn't have been surprised if they'd gone in circles. There were steps up and down, and Emma wasn't sure if they were upstairs, on the ground floor, or in a basement. They'd probably not gone that far, but Emma decided she was totally lost.

The large kitchen had flagstone floors like one of those National Trust kind of places. Shelves lined one wall and housed several large copper and iron pans. A single lamp in the corner illuminated a large kitchen clock and the edge of a large solid top cooking range.

"I'm sorry. It's a bit like a working museum," Maggie apologized

It certainly looked old, and well used. "I like it here, it's warm, and…nice."

Maggie glanced about the room as though for the first time. "I suppose so. It's been the kitchen for many generations."

Emma wandered around. The table in the middle of the room could seat eight or ten people at a time. Two sunken ceramic sinks stood under a long window with stone mullions and a wide stone window sill.

When she noticed that the kitchen wrapped around the corner into an L-shaped space, she couldn't help but take a peek. Weak lighting, presumably from a generator, illuminated more shelves, another sink, and lots of plates piled upon open shelves. A cupboard stretched from floor to ceiling. One of the doors stood slightly ajar, and she could see the glint of light off cans and jars. It was probably a pantry, then.

Maggie rummaged through a fridge so old it was very nearly antique. "Cheese. Ham. Paté. Home-made pickles. Bread and crackers. Does that sound all right?"

"It sounds fantastic," Emma replied.

"Good," Maggie said, and she loaded her choices onto a

trolley. "A little bit of this and a little bit of that." She hummed as she worked her way through the food items. "Red or white?"

"White?"

"Good choice." She piled plates and glasses onto the trolley next to the food.

"No tea?"

Maggie stopped what she was doing. "Tea?"

Emma laughed. "Joking. The wine sounds perfect."

"Thank goodness." Maggie added olives to the feast on the trolley. "I think this will do it, don't you?"

"How many are coming?"

"Do you think I've got too much?"

"Not at all. I think there's enough for me, but what are you having?"

"Ha ha! Smart aleck."

10

RELAXING

E mma slipped off her shoes and curled up on one of the
worn but comfortable wingback chairs. The heat from
the open fire turned her all nice and toasty. She glanced
towards Maggie, the lord of Magwood, who was nothing like
she'd expected. If only Barbara were here to see this.

"Are you comfortable?" Maggie asked. She regarded
Emma over the rim of her glass.

Any thoughts of anything outside of the here and now
vanished. Had Maggie seen her stare?

Emma brushed her hand against the distressed leather.
"Don't tell me. This is an original piece, an antique and worth
a fortune?"

"Would you be concerned if I said it was?"

"Of course I would. I'm sitting in the chair as though…"
She hesitated.

"As though what?" Maggie prompted.

"I'm slouched all over it as though I'm familiar with
sitting here. I shouldn't though, and I shouldn't be such a slob
on something old and expensive."

"You look comfortable. You must bear in mind that in this

house, very little is new. Those chairs have been there since long before I was born."

"Then they're not old, they're ancient."

"Cheeky." Maggie chuckled. She rose from her seat and pulled the trolley a little closer.

Emma blushed. "I didn't mean it like that. In here, I'm surrounded by the kinds of things that normal people would never buy."

"Normal? What do you mean by normal?"

"I mean regular people. Not lords and stuff."

"So you think I'm not normal?"

"Now you're trying to twist things."

Maggie laughed. "Yes, I am."

"Should we be sitting on it?"

"What? The chair? Of course, that's what it's there for."

"But it might be worth something. It could be valuable. Normal people don't—"

"It's worth sitting on, that's what it is worth," Maggie interrupted. She poured two more glasses of wine and handed one to Emma. "Now, never mind my chairs. Tell me about yourself. How much do you know about your aunt?"

"Aren't you supposed to be answering *my* questions? You said you would."

"Later. Humor me, please."

"All right."

"Tell me what you know about your aunt."

Emma took a sip of wine. "My great aunt, really, and I didn't even know she existed until I had a visit from a solicitor a few weeks ago. I think you know more about her than I do."

"Do I?"

"Well, I'm adopted, and I grew up as Emma Blewitt. Until a few weeks ago, I'd never even heard of the Tappers or Castlecoombe."

"I see. So tell me about yourself."

"You are an inquisitive one, aren't you?"

Maggie laughed. "We're neighbors now, and it is my duty as lord of this manor to know everyone."

"So it's like a job interview, then?" she asked,

"I'm out of practice. I don't get many visitors."

"I see. My parents, my biological parents, died when I was young, and as a result, I spent time in a number of homes and institutions. People prefer to adopt babies, you see, not grown kids, so my future looked bleak. I moved from care home to foster home, and back to care homes."

"That must have been very disheartening."

"You have no idea," Emma said. "Then along came the Blewitts. They were an older couple, so they'd never be given a young baby."

"That sounds unfair."

Emma shrugged. "The whole system is unfair, but everyone tries their best, I suppose." Her voice trailed off as her memories of the homes came back to her.

"Then what happened?" Maggie prompted.

"The Blewitts were lovely from the get-go, I'd been in foster care for long enough to appreciate people who showed genuine concern."

"How long were you in the system for?" Maggie asked.

"Three years."

"A long time for a child."

"Yes, and it was difficult for a while, but my mom and dad made sure I understood where I came from and helped me to make decisions about my life. They were supportive and encouraging even when I decided to look for my biological family."

"They sound lovely."

"Yes, I loved them to bits," Emma said. She stared into the fire, but the glow of the logs didn't seem to make her feel warm. A coldness settled into her bones. She shook off the feeling with a shiver. "Anyway, we spent a lot of time and money trying to find anyone we could."

"What happened?"

"I didn't find anything, if that's what you mean. Everyone I found was dead."

"That must have been upsetting."

"Not really. It was a shame, that's for sure, but it was easy to accept then. I loved my parents and they loved me—what more could I ask for?" She smiled, but it was a sad smile. "It was a big surprise to find I had an aunt. It was even more of a surprise to learn she had been looking for me."

"You loved them? Past tense?"

"Yes. Everyone has passed on now."

"I'm sorry."

"No need. These things happen."

"I know, but still, it must have been tough."

"It makes me sad sometimes. I was born, then my parents died. A couple adopted me, and they died. Then I discovered I had an aunt, but she's already dead. My past is littered with deceased relatives." She sighed. "It's such a shame, and it could all have been avoided."

"How so?"

"Blame it on my grandmother, I suppose. She wanted to do a disappearing act and no one seems to know why. I know she didn't want to be a Tapper, but I can only guess why when I have so little to go on." She stared at the wine in her glass, her mind wandering for a moment. "Perhaps now I'm here, I'll be able to find out what was so horrible about being a Tapper."

Maggie rested her hand upon Emma's fire-warmed fingers and squeezed gently, but she didn't say anything.

Emma stared at their hands. Pleasant little zaps of electricity shot between them, and she wondered if they could be seen, or whether it was all in her imagination.

"Sometimes," she continued, "I fear that no matter where I

go, I am destined to lose people the moment I find them. I will go through life leaving a string of bodies behind me. I shall be alone forever, I think."

Emma felt shocked by her own words. She hadn't meant to be so open, but there was something about Maggie that made her feel safe.

"You sound so cynical for one so young," Maggie said.

"That doesn't make it any less valid."

"True. Look on the bright side, though. You had wonderful parents that you adored. Not everyone can claim that much."

"I suppose."

"And now that you're here, you can take as much time as you want to find out about your family history."

Emma stared into the fire a moment longer. "You're right. Anyway, enough about me, what about you?"

"What to say? My life until now has been nothing special."

"Nothing special? Goodness. A beautiful woman with a title and an ancestral home, your suitors must be queuing from here to the Inger to see you."

Maggie snorted. "No one rushes to attach themselves to my name or my family. Even if they did want to see me, I would not be interested."

"Why?" Emma asked, intrigued. Then she stopped. "I'm sorry, I'm being nosey. It's like I've known you for years already, and I feel almost as though I'm supposed to be here."

Maggie looked at her, as though searching for an answer. "Strange, isn't it?"

"Must be what comes of having a gun waved at me."

"I'm sorry. Would it help if I said the gun wasn't loaded?"

Emma stared at Maggie for a moment and then laughed. "Perhaps I should shoot you for scaring me for no reason."

"And leave another body behind?"

Maggie's words shocked Emma to the core. Her eyes started to water, but she held them back.

"I think I'm done leaving bodies," she whispered.

11

MIDNIGHT COMES

Maggie smiled to herself as she showed Emma back to the guest room. They had talked such a great deal, but she was glad that she had been able to sidestep some of the more awkward questions. It wasn't that she really wanted to deceive, but sometimes real life was too complicated and too weird to talk about.

"Here you are, all safe and sound."

"Thank you, Maggie. I don't think I would have found it by myself."

She leaned against the wall with as much nonchalance as she could muster. "No problem. I said I would keep you out of trouble."

"You did."

"I've had a wonderful evening. Thank you."

Emma fiddled with her watch. "I've had a great evening, too. You're so kind to take me in and spoil me like this. It's almost as though it had all been planned this way."

"It would be very spooky if it had been."

Emma looked up at Maggie with a cheeky grin. "I'd offer you a nightcap, but I think we had plenty downstairs."

Maggie laughed. "You're probably right." She waited a

moment, but Emma stood there, her hand on the door handle and the storm torch set to glow in her hand. "Perhaps it is time to go. Goodnight, Emma. Sleep well."

Emma smiled back and put her hand on Maggie's arm. "Goodnight," she whispered, but her voice was so low and soft that Maggie leaned forward. Next, she felt Emma's lips brush against her cheek. "Sleep well." The door to the room opened, and Emma slipped inside. "See you in the morning.".

"If you need anything, I'm down the corridor."

"Okay. Thank you," Emma answered, and shut the door, slowly. Maggie could almost say that she closed the door reluctantly. It was a nice thought, really, and even if it was nothing more than hopefulness, it filled her with a warm glow. So much so that she ignored the chill of the house as she made her way to her own room.

In the cold, she rushed through her preparations for bed and slipped between the sheets. She lay on her back and waited for sleep to come.

When it didn't, she stared at the ceiling. Maybe sleep evaded her because there was a Tapper in the house.

A Tapper! Who'd have thought! How was it even possible, given the history of the families? Well, she knew the reason for that.

Emma Tapper, or rather Emma Blewitt, was an interesting woman. She was everything Maggie had dreamed of and then some. More than those dark Tapper eyes and that dark beauty, this one had a gentle heart not present in any Tapper she'd ever known.

Maggie raised tentative fingers to her cheek. The imprint of Emma's lips still burned against her skin. Her stomach flipped so hard she whimpered. This was not the right time to find herself getting close to anyone, never mind a Tapper, but she couldn't help herself.

She was tired, she supposed. And fed up of being alone. One pleasant evening wasn't too much to ask for, was it?

The first drop of cold water landed in the middle of her forehead.

The second landed on the bridge of her nose. She turned to look at the clock on her bedside table and the third drop landed below her ear.

The clock, an old two-bell ringer older than she was, read a quarter after twelve. Maggie closed her eyes and waited.

The temperature dropped even further, and when she peered through half-lidded eyes, her breath shot out in small cones of steam. She was glad she used a duvet and several blankets at night, but then, she was used to these nocturnal visits.

"Come on, then," she breathed. Nothing and no one was going to upset her now. Her evening had been too perfect.

"Do you…Do you…" the disembodied voice echoed through her room.

"No," she whispered in wispy breaths of steam. She touched her cheek once more. "I don't know."

12

WHEN CHARLES MET A WEASEL

Charles Durrant woke up in his usual hotel room and stretched. A quiet knock at the door caught his attention.

"Enter," he said.

A young man in hotel livery unlocked the door and slipped into the room.

"Breakfast, sir," he said, as he placed a tray on the small table in the corner.

Charles was gratified to note how the young man moved without making noise, and he handled the tray like a professional. There was no irritating clinking of chinaware or cutlery. Perfect.

"Thank you," Charles said. He contemplated a tip, but the young man left before he could move to locate his wallet. The door closed with a gentle sigh and locked with a soft *ker-thunk*.

"Charles," a sleep-filled voice mumbled beside him.

"Time to get up," he said, as he swung his legs over the side. "Shower, if you like, whilst I have my breakfast."

"Any for me?" she asked. "I could do with a coffee."

"I didn't order you anything." He wrapped his dressing

gown around his body as she got out of bed. "Don't dawdle. I have a busy day."

He poured himself a cup of coffee, settled behind his morning paper, and in spite of any noises she made as she got dressed, paid her no attention. He had already forgotten she existed, and her movements became a part of the background noise.

"Will I see you later, hun?" she asked, and paused at the door.

Charles scowled at such presumption of intimacy. "I'll call you," he answered. His tone of voice was quite brusque, even for him. He didn't care much. "Bye."

As the door closed, he settled into the familiar comforts of his paper and breakfast. His attention didn't waver from the printed pages, except when he needed to refill his coffee cup. Now and then, his mind wandered from the stark misery of the news, and drifted towards the pleasurable contemplation of the day ahead. He scanned the racing news, but this was not a racing day. Not today.

A knock at the door drew his daydreams to a halt. He checked his watch. He didn't yet expect the maid service, and, annoyed he had been disturbed, controlled his irritation with great effort.

He opened the door. "Yes?" he hissed

Outside the room, a man slouched against the corridor wall. With both hands shoved deep into his pockets, he looked at odds with the fine surroundings of this hotel. With his hunched posture, his head seemed to protrude from his chest rather than off his neck, and greasy lank hair covered his face and eyes. His clothes were far from pristine, but the man looked familiar nonetheless.

Charles scowled. "Yes?" He searched for the man's name, but none came to him.

The man inclined his head. "It's me, my lord. Weasel. As in Catweasel. Come for me money."

"Good God, man, do you not understand English? I said not here. Never here, no matter what."

"It's important," Weasel whined.

"How the hell did you get by the security guards?"

"The fire escape." Weasel grinned, and it was not a pretty sight. "Folk leave windows open all over the place, you know."

Charles checked to make sure no one was looking and waved the man in. "Very well, come in, seeing as I don't have much choice."

Sly eyes peered around the whole room. "Nice," Weasel said. He sniffed the air as though evaluating the worth of the place through his sense of smell.

"Don't even think about stealing anything."

"No. I won't. Nowt here worth anything."

"Right." Charles wrinkled his nose. "What's that smell?"

Weasel gripped his wrinkled shirt below the collar and sniffed himself. "Dunno. Slept with the dog in the back of the car the last few nights. Maybe it's the dog you smell."

"Good lord, man, get yourself washed and cleaned so you smell like a person, not a dirty animal."

Weasel shrugged.

"Well, make it fast, then. You stink to high heaven. They'll need to fumigate the room afterwards."

"So, I have to be here 'cause the boss—you know the boss, Mister Orsen. The one from the Broadway Casino? The same one you owe all of that money to? He wants his money, and he don't like waiting none. He says he's waited long enough already. He gave you enough credit as is."

Charles pulled himself upright. "Everyone will get paid once I am lord of Magwood Hall and Castlecoombe proper. You know this. I have explained it many times. How many more will I need to say it?" Charles walked to the hotel window and stared outside. "The situation will not change while my sister is around. To inherit what is mine, she must no longer be an issue. Of course, she wouldn't be an issue if someone did what they were paid to do."

"I ain't been paid."

"I'm not paying a fool who can't keep his end of the deal."

"Not my fault. Not my fault."

"Yes, you sniveling little slime ball. It is. You promised."

"I don't know why you're in such a rush…sir," he added as an afterthought. "Last week you said she was gonna die soon anyway. Why don't you wait until then? It would be safer."

"Yes. She will die of the family curse." He snorted. "They always die."

Weasel shook his head. "So what's the rush?"

"Because it's mine, and I want it now. I'm not about to rely on some ancient mumbo jumbo for my money. She might live a year more, and I don't want to wait." He smiled with eyes like a glacier. "I will give you twenty-four hours to remedy this pitiful situation. Don't worry about your money. You'll get it when the job is done and not a minute before." He thought for a moment. "In fact, if you sort out this little problem sooner rather than later, I'll give you a bonus. Are you interested?"

Weasel's eyes narrowed. "Keep talking."

"Ahh, good man. I like a fellow who understands such matters."

"How soon do you want it done? I need a day or two to get ready."

"Very wise," Charles said. He nodded. "Prepare to act in two days. I'll call to verify, of course, because I need to be out of the way and with a good alibi."

"And the bonus? How much of a bonus would you be willing to pay?"

"I don't know." Charles scratched his chin in thought. "How about as much silverware as you can carry in a small bag?"

"Like a small rucksack?"

"That would be about the right size, yes."

"And how would that work out?"

"Just help yourself to whatever takes your fancy in the main hall. There's a collection of antique snuff boxes in a cabinet. Must be worth a small fortune, I should say. Perhaps silver platters take your fancy, so take a look in the dining room."

Weasel's eyes lit up.

"You find yourself a nice spot, and come evening, you could deal with her as you saw fit. She goes to bed early so do with her what you will. A good man like you should be able to sort her out, I'm sure. Then *deal* with her."

Weasel's eyes almost popped out of his head, and he grinned. It wasn't a pretty sight, and no matter what he did to his face, his looks would never improve much. "I can do whatever I like? Anything?"

"Yes. Telephone the police after you leave so they can be the ones to find her. I need to have an alibi in town. Do you understand what I'm saying?"

Weasel shrugged.

"Do we have an understanding, my good fellow?"

"I think we do."

"Good. Now until then, get the hell out of my sight."

Alone, Charles stared at the door. The smell of Weasel hung about, but he'd smelled worse on the farm. A short pang of guilt brought his delicate brows together, but he shook it off. She was his sister, and he was a little concerned about arranging unpleasant things for her, but she had his money. So it was her fault, really.

His mood lifted and his guilt ended, Charles drained his cup of coffee. It was cold, but he didn't care. "This is going to be marvelous day. I can feel it in my bones."

He laughed. Everything was coming together. He knew it. His sister would no longer be a problem. That would be the main thing. It didn't matter what that odious little man stole, either; it was all registered, and the fool didn't have a clue about antiques or how to get rid of them discreetly. He would be caught selling stolen goods, Charles would get his belongings back, and the police would wonder if the thief was also the murderer. No point paying money to someone in prison, was there?

He smiled. With things looking this good, he deserved to get himself a new suit. His luck had changed, and when luck changed, a clever man made the most of it. And if Weasel failed, he had a trick or two up his sleeve to make sure his luck stayed changed.

13

MAUD'S HOUSE IN DAYLIGHT

Emma rose early to find herself in a strange room. It looked so different in the rays of sunshine that streamed through the opened curtains. She'd thought she'd closed them the night before, but maybe she hadn't after all. She found a note slipped under the door.

Hope you slept well. I had an early start and didn't want to disturb you.

Help yourself to the shower and facilities. Same with breakfast in the kitchen.

Hope you have a better day than you did yesterday. Castlecoombe is a good place. You'll see.

There is a key in the kitchen door so you can lock up. I'll get it from you later.

Maggie.

PS. I enjoyed last night. We should do it again. If you want?

E mma took advantage of all of the offered facilities, and showered whilst standing in an ancient clawfoot tub that stood in a huge bathroom. It was nice. Warm sunlight streamed through the windows, and a large potted plant in the corner glistened with reflected sunlight.

After that, she decided the note also included an invitation to look around a little more. At least the ground floor. The rest she thought of as private and personal.

The hall where they'd shared a meal and a bottle of wine looked different during the day. Warm sunlight streamed through the tall windows, and the mullions and transoms cast delightful shadows across the floor. Outside, the clear, cloudless blue sky promised a warm, pleasant day. Emma's mood rose with an influx of hope and the possibilities of a new house and a new day.

She sat in the same wingback chair she'd sat in last night. The fireplace had been swept and cleaned. Yes, she could still feel the warmth of the fire in the remnants of logs and coals, but she had no idea what to do with it. Not that she could stay here all day. She leaned back and closed her eyes.

What an adventure.

She shivered, and goosebumps erupted along her arms. It appeared to be such a nice day, and with so much sunshine, yet she felt cold. She wrapped her arms around herself and noted that puffs of steam jetted out with every breath. It was time to leave.

In the kitchen, she grabbed a slice of bread and ham, just to see her through. She fancied a coffee, too, but one look around the kitchen told her she didn't know where to start. On the wall, a large clock, pitted and discolored with age, looked like one of those clocks that designers called shabby chic. In other words, cheap tat made to look antique.

Tick.

She stared at the clock and waited. It didn't look tacky and cheap, though.

Tock.

This was Magwood Hall. Nothing here was cheap and tacky. Most of what she'd seen had been old. That being the case, even this clock had to be a true antique.

She left the hall and drove down to Maud's house. In daylight, with the sun out and any sign of the storm long gone, the village looked more inviting than it had the previous night. Then, in the darkness and rain, she'd thought the village to be tiny. Now that she could see further, she realized there was more to Castlecoombe than a few houses nestled around a small, but well-tended green.

The tree at the heart of this small common ground looked as gnarled and deformed as it had first appeared. The twisted branches clawed at the sky, as though to stave off the brightness of day. There were several side roads, and although she itched to take a better look at the area, the village would be here later. First, she had a house to look at.

Maud's house, like most of the nearby houses, had been constructed from local stone. The dark grey blocks looked dour and miserable no matter what the weather. Even in the sunshine, the house looked dark and unappealing. Now, though, it appeared dark with a sense of sadness rather than menace, and the dancing, light-sucking shadows were nowhere to be seen.

The small front garden, overgrown with nettles, thistles, and other weeds, completed the look of abandonment. A climbing rose surrounded the door, but it had grown thin and diseased from lack of care. She wondered what it would look like if pruned and cared for. She'd always wanted a front door with roses growing beside it.

Thus encouraged, Emma took a few deep breaths of the clear air, and with each breath, it seemed as though she expelled the last remains of city pollution from her lungs.

She turned to look at the houses nearby. A few curtains twitched, but no one stepped out to greet her. Not that she'd expected any kind of welcome. After all, she'd spent most of her adult life in the city, where keeping to oneself was a survival mechanism. This would be no different. Except that village folk were supposed to be friendly, weren't they?

At the doorstep, she reached into one of the side pockets of her bag to fish out Maud's keys. Her fingers wrapped around the one to the kitchen at Magwood Hall, instead. She stared at the little key for a moment, and then looked back towards the hall. Sunlight glinted from the parts of the gatehouse that were still intact. It looked magnificent. Halfway up the mountainside, Magwood Hall, more castle than hall, overlooked the valley and town with an air of desolation. There were several towers, all with witch-hat roofs and crenelated walls. One tower stood out more than others, protruding from the wall over the valley itself. It looked almost crooked. Emma smiled at the sight. The imperfection made the place more appealing in some way.

"Maggie Durrant," Emma said to herself. "I'd date you just to get inside your castle again." Then she laughed as she thought about an evening spent in front of a roaring fire drinking wine and talking late into the night. "Problem is, I'd date you if you were the girl next door, too."

She shook off her thoughts and searched for the right key. With rather more enthusiasm than the first time she had stood on the threshold, Emma unlocked the door and entered the house.

It was still dark inside, but this time when she flicked the light switch, a single bulb lit the hall with a pale yellow glow.

"Hot damn. We have lift off."

The unopened mail spread across the floor in an untidy mess, some even had signs of her wet footprints. She stepped over the mail, closed the door, and looked about the downstairs area with a critical eye. Despair rose like a tide. There was so much to do.

Get a grip, she told herself. Might as well get on with it.

Emma bustled into the kitchen and dropped her bag on one of the chairs. She used the small table as the center of operations and unloaded various items from her small carry all bag onto the table.

She opened a notepad and grabbed a pen. Her first job, she reckoned, would be to go into each room and assess what she had to do. She had brought some things with her, but her car, small as it was, couldn't hold too much in the way of supplies or equipment.

At the back of the kitchen, a door led to a pantry tucked under the slope of the staircase. Amongst the rest of the items stored there, she found an old but functional vacuum cleaner, brushes, a mop, and a bucket. Equipped with the other cleaning materials she'd thought to stuff into her car, Emma had more than enough to get started. Now to look around the house.

A lack of central heating was not the only feature of modern living Emma found missing. There was no television, and the radio, not attuned to digital broadcasts, produced an abundance of static but nothing else. The furniture looked old and worn, but not all of it antique. When she patted the sofa, she wiped her hand down her jeans to remove the damp grit that clung to her skin.

Did Maud never clean? she wondered, then took herself to task. It was unfair to judge someone she didn't know, and she knew it. Maggie had already told her old Maud Tapper had spent some time in a nursing home, and the chances were she was not capable of doing much when she was home.

A pang of sadness stopped her in her tracks. Poor Maud had been alone. She'd had no one to help, and with no one to turn to, both she and the house had suffered.

Emma wondered whether this house showed her what life alone would look like in her future. Was this all she had to look forward to? The picture didn't look appealing. She'd never met anyone she'd cared for enough to settle down. She didn't seem to want the same things as anyone she'd dated so far. She didn't want to go out every night. She wanted to sit by the fire and… Her thoughts drifted. And talk to someone like she had last night. It was an appealing thought, but lords were out of her league for a start.

Loneliness might well figure in her future, as it had Maud's later years, but this was not an empty house. Despite the lack of modern comforts Emma had expected, this was a home, not a house. There were pictures and paintings of people on every surface. She found a whole history spread out on the walls. Her entire lineage, a genealogist's dream, laid out for all to see. Sadness washed over her in drowning waves until she shook her head.

"You're all my family," she said with determination, "and I will know you all."

Upstairs, the rooms were in a time-distressed state, but Emma was no longer so judgmental.

"Poor Maud," she said to the walls. "I wish I had known you. I would have come, and you would not have been alone." A whisper, or an echo, whirled like smoke from room to room, and Emma smiled; the house agreed with her. It was the right thing to say.

14

A VISITOR

Emma knew, without need of a mirror, that she did not look her best. Once she'd started cleaning, she'd changed into a pair of old jogging bottoms. They were stained, saggy, misshapen, and they did not make her rear look good. An oversized tee shirt with assorted stains and bleach marks added to her frumpy shapeless look, but at least she wouldn't ruin any of the few nice clothes she'd brought with her.

If that wasn't enough, she completed the look with Maud's bright floral pinafore apron. She didn't know how old it was, but knowing how trends went, this particular design was sure to have been retro at least twice already. It was a substantial item of wear, and it wrapped around her body and covered her from neck to knee in great grandmother fashion. She scrutinized herself in the mirror as she tied her hair back yet again with an old cloth, and the startled scarecrow, with dirt smudges across her cheek, stared back at her. Emma didn't care, and when she heard a knock, she dismissed it as a neighbor come to be nosey. She opened the door anyway.

"Hello," Maggie said as she held a brown bag in the air. "I come bearing gifts of sustenance."

"You're a treasure. Come in."

"You look great."

"Don't be a smart-arse, Maggie. I look like crap."

"That's not true at all. You look cute and attractive in a housewifey kind of way."

Emma stopped what she was doing. "Did you just call me cute? And attractive?"

Maggie froze for a moment and looked away. "How's it going?" she asked, as though to avoid the question. She unloaded a couple of cheese baguettes, a tub of coleslaw, salad, and two cups of coffee.

Emma let the comment pass. For the moment. "Good. There's no heating, but there is so much to do that I don't have time to get cold. I would freeze if I had to sit down and do nothing."

"We'll get the heating sorted out for you soon."

"I know."

"Have you adjusted to being here yet?"

"In part, but it's so weird."

"How so?"

Emma looked around as though seeking inspiration for her thoughts. "For a start, everything is so old. I swear it's a 1950s museum rather than a home. Sometimes, I feel like I'm trespassing. Then other times, it feels kinda snug, as if I fit, and I'm supposed to be here."

"Well, you can't trespass in your own house. It's all strange and new. Perhaps it'll be better when you have your own things here. You know, there are collectors who would love some of these antiques. There's an auction house in Moorville. It's a big town, and you'd have driven through on the way here. I'm sure they'd be able to sort you out with a good price for things."

"What a good idea. Thanks for that."

"I also have a number for the oil company, but I don't think they'll come to fill your tank for a few days. They're not fast at the best of times, but with winter around the corner, best do it now rather than wait."

"Fantastic. You've been so helpful. I couldn't manage without you. How can I repay you?"

Maggie looked bashful for a moment. "Have dinner with me tonight?" She looked into Emma's eyes. "Say yes."

"Well…"

"This place isn't ready for you, so stay the night at the hall. I would love your company again. I had such a fabulous time last night, and I can't miss the opportunity to repeat it."

"You really want to repeat it?"

Maggie laughed. "I do. It was fun."

Emma didn't have to think long. "I would be honored. Can I bring anything? Do anything?"

"No, it's fine. But now I'm here, you could show me around the house. I'd love to know what the Tapper museum looks like when the lighting is good."

Emma laughed. "It's filthy. I touched the sofa, and it felt like grit stuck to my hand."

"Your aunt was in a nursing home for a long time, and no one has been here since."

"So much for community spirit," Emma observed.

"Unfair. We're all simple folk here. Private. We don't interfere."

"I have seen curtains twitching. They do like to watch."

"They're keeping an eye out."

"What for?" Emma asked.

"Anything untoward," Maggie replied.

"Right."

"How's your progress with things?"

"Slow. You know, it is going to take me ages to clean this place up and make it ready to sell," Emma said, wiping her finger over several surfaces. "And the dust and grime…I'll be cleaning it up for weeks." She tried, with varying degrees of success, to stop herself from wiping every surface she passed.

"You've decided to leave?"

"Yes, of course. Why would I stay here when my place is in the city? I work there, and the house will give me enough money to make home ownership less painful there."

"Of course." Yet Maggie couldn't stop the hint of disappointment from creeping into her voice. "It would be cheaper to live here, though."

"Yes, it would, but there's no work for me here. And it's not exactly a communications hub. I'm not sure my phone has worked once since I got here."

"I understand," Maggie said. The disappointment in her voice was even stronger.

Emma sighed. "To be honest, I have no idea what I'm doing. I had so many plans when I started out, and now I'm not so sure."

"Those plans were to sell up?"

"Yes. But it's different here. I think I'd like to get a better feel for the place and just absorb it, you know?"

Maggie nodded, but she said nothing.

"I had family here. It seems unfair to run away when I've just found them. I think I'm home here, and that sounds very strange."

"She had a lot of memories here, your aunt. And the family has lived here for generations."

"Yes, I know. It's fascinating to be able to look back so far."

"Were you not intrigued by these relations of yours before you left the city?"

Emma considered the question for a moment. "Yes. At first, I wanted to know them, to know who they were, and I admit I was quite desperate. But then a part of me said I had been alone all this time; it wouldn't make any difference to seek them out now. They're gone."

"I'm sorry. It must be difficult," Maggie sympathized.

"Yes. Let me show you," she said, drawing Maggie into the lounge and pointing at the many pictures and portraits hanging on the wall. She stood in front of one particular painting. "Agnes Tapper," she read from the label. "An ancestor, and not so far back in the scheme of things, and yet I know nothing about her. There are others, all here, but they're strangers to me. A part of me is sad because I don't know them and never will." She stared at the pictures. "There's no point in missing something I can never replace. I wasn't a part of their lives, and I owe them nothing. Perhaps, given time, I might feel differently, but for now, I'm not sure how I'm supposed to react to any of it." She shrugged. "Do I seem cold and uncaring?"

"No, of course not. It will take time to sort things out here. Perhaps your feelings will change when you soak up the family spirit."

"You look disappointed in me, Maggie."

"I'm not disappointed in you."

"Then what is it?"

"Nothing."

"There's most certainly something." Emma reached out. "Tell me."

"I know it's only been a day since we met, but, well, it's like I've known you all my life. Is that strange?" Maggie rolled her shoulders as though steeling herself to speak. "If you stay long enough, then you might find more reasons to stay."

"Such as?"

"I don't know. The family. Your house. The village, and the countryside around here. You might like it." She stared at her hands as she twiddled her thumbs. "Then you'd stay longer, and I'd get to enjoy your company."

"Then we shall see."

"We shall," Maggie echoed.

Emma stared at Maggie for a moment and turned back to

the display on the wall. "I keep looking at these pictures. It's so strange, standing here, surrounded by these strangers who look like me." She turned her attention to a picture on the opposite wall, where a middle-aged woman with light brown hair and unexceptional looks stared back. Unexceptional but for her dark eyes, and they stared out with such intensity, they left Emma stripped to the core. She recognized those eyes; she saw them every time she looked in a mirror.

"Maud Tapper, your aunt," Maggie said. "When she was younger."

"She is—was—a striking woman," Emma said. "Scary, too."

"I didn't know her very well. She kept to herself."

"Perhaps the house should have been left to you. I think you're more interested than I am."

Maggie laughed. "I don't think so, Emma. I think you want to know, too. I have an advantage. Our families have been here a long time, and I grew up knowing about everyone."

"Everyone?"

"Well, pretty much."

They looked at all the pictures in the room, all of them members of the Tapper family, sometimes with their partners. "I have the same eyes as most of the people in these pictures, don't I?"

"Yes, you have very distinctive Tapper eyes," Maggie said.

"There are more pictures along the stairs and in the bedrooms. Did you want to take a look?"

Maggie nodded enthusiastically. "Yes, I do. Until you came along, I'd never been inside Maud's house. This is really fascinating."

Emma smiled. "Come upstairs, then. There are so many pictures everywhere, and maybe you can tell me who they were."

"I'll do my best."

They only managed to get halfway up the stairs when Maggie stopped. "You were right. There are a lot of pictures. The resemblances between the women of the Tapper family are remarkable. It helps that some of them are labelled, I have to say."

"I know. I'm so glad my aunt, or whoever, had the foresight to put information on the bottom, at least on some of them. At least I know when the pictures were taken, sketched, or painted, and who was in each."

"Your aunt was very organized."

"As I said, she made it like a look like a museum."

"You could probably work out your family tree from the information on the walls alone."

"A few generations at least," Emma said. She stared at one of the sepia-toned pictures of a young man with Tapper eyes. His wife had pale eyes, but their son had the same color eyes as his dad. "Tapper eyes," she whispered to the photograph.

"There you go." Maggie grinned. "You're halfway to understanding your ancestors."

Goosebumps erupted along Emma's arms, and she shivered.

"You're cold. Do you want my fleecy jacket?" Maggie offered.

"Then you'll get cold."

"I have a jumper underneath." Maggie draped her coat over Emma's shoulders. "Better?"

The coat surrounded Emma in warmth. "I wish I had central heating. Then I wouldn't freeze upstairs, and I could look around a little bit more. It's not so bad when I'm working—moving keeps me quite toasty. But up here, I freeze."

"You could wear a coat."

"It's supposed to be warmer inside than out."

"The house has been locked up for a while without heat. Why didn't you light a fire, at least downstairs?"

"I was busy so I didn't notice too much downstairs."

"Ahh right, Still, once you get a fire going, the heat will circulate round and make the whole place warmer. And you'll get a little warmth from the main chimney to warm upstairs as well."

"There are fireplaces everywhere. Will I have to light them all?"

"Probably. Is there one in the master bedroom?"

Emma led the way. In the corner of the master bedroom stood a fireplace. Blackened with use and filled with wood ash, it was one more thing that hadn't been cleaned in a while.

"There you go, the heating system," Maggie said.

Emma reached under the nightstand and pulled out a small fan heater. "It looks like Maud gave up on the fire as well."

"A fire can be a nuisance first thing of a cold morning, especially if you don't get the hang of banking it overnight," Maggie admitted. "And it might be quite awkward for you until you get used to it."

Emma nodded. "If I'm going to stay here, then I'll get central heating installed."

Maggie grinned and turned her attention to the rest of the room.

"She had good furniture," Emma noted. The walnut wood wardrobe and matching dresser would be popular in those trendy shops hidden away in the expensive parts of town. She might keep the set herself; they looked good, were in reasonable condition, and looked a lot nicer than the chipboard rubbish owned.

Pictures covered the walls here, too, but above the fireplace were two paintings covered in dusty sheets. She grabbed the edge of one sheet and pulled it off one of the pictures, then did the same for the other.

They were paintings, both of them, and unlike the

photographs and sketches found in the rest of the house. These were older, and more like an old master's work in a portrait gallery. They were large and imposing with small gilt frames, and now that they were uncovered, they dominated the room. It wasn't so much the artwork that made her stare, but the subject of the paintings. "What is this?"

From the sound of Maggie's indrawn breath, she had seen them, too.

"Would you take a look at those beauties?" she said.

A number of wild thoughts ran through Emma's mind, but the most dominant emotion was confusion. "I can't believe my eyes. This is incredible." She turned to Maggie at her side. "Maggie?"

Maggie stared at the pictures, "Yes?"

"Why is there a picture of you in my aunt's bedroom?" Emma asked.

Maggie's voice grew hoarse. "I could ask the same thing. The other picture is the spitting image of you."

"It's not me, it's just the eyes. You said yourself, Tapper eyes are very distinctive." She looked at Maggie out of the corner of her eye. "We Tappers all look alike, you know."

Maggie snorted. "Now I think you're trying to pull my leg."

"Maybe."

"Anyway, that's not it. Look closer."

Emma looked. Tapper eyes, for sure, and they drew you in until you failed to look at anything else. "I'm not sure."

"Well," Maggie started, and her gaze shifted from Emma's face to the portrait. "The shape of the face is identical, more so than any of the other Tappers, who have more rounded faces. Your cheekbones and hers are more prominent than most of the Tapper pictures I've seen. Even your hair color and style are similar, although yours is shorter."

Emma looked at the portrait, and there was no denying the fact that the face in the painting was a close match to the face she saw in the mirror every day. "All right," she admitted. "I see the resemblance."

"Good."

"That's all very well. Me being a Tapper and all that, it's expected."

"Yes," Maggie agreed.

"But what the hell is a picture of you doing in my aunt's room? These old faces are yours and mine. Why?"

"Obviously, it's not me, but I suppose the family resemblances have passed down my line, the same as yours."

"This is too weird, you know."

"I know!" Maggie grinned, though, and her long fingers caressed the side of one of the frames. "This is so amazing. You don't know how much."

"Then tell me."

"It's a long story, generations in the making, and these pictures are not supposed to exist."

"Do you mean they were never supposed to have existed —or never supposed to have survived?"

"You make a valid point. Many of my ancestors have argued that these pictures do not exist. But here they are, and so they were wrong."

"You don't seem all that surprised, though."

"No, I'm not surprised that they exist, but I'm very surprised to find them, most of all to find them here." She stroked the paint work close to the frame. "Really, this is special. When I researched the family, I was convinced that they existed, even though no one had any proof of them."

"Why did you think they existed?"

Maggie stopped still. "Hints, mostly. A comment here and there about images and likenesses, and in the distant past, a couple of artists have been commissioned and yet I can't find their work. Either they were sold or lost. That's where we get the arguments for the two portraits."

"And here we are."

"Indeed. Here we are, and I am the first one to see them." She shook her head, "I still can't believe they exist."

"So, if it isn't you?"

"That's where it gets interesting."

"I think you'd better give me the short version, then."

Maggie laughed. "I think it's my great-great-great-great grandfather, give or take a few greats, Charles Magwood Durrant. He has very fine and delicate features for a man."

"And the other picture?"

"Well, she would be Emily Tapper."

"My aunt?"

"Emily Tapper would be your great-great-great-great-great grandmother, or something like that, and the resemblance between you is more amazing than I could have imagined. It's like she's reborn."

"So you must be Charles reborn?"

Maggie chuckled, but she didn't answer.

"Anyway, why are these pictures in my aunt's bedroom?"

"It's a long story."

"Another one? You do like your long stories, Maggie Durrant."

"Yes, but it's cold in here. I'd rather be comfortable when I start talking. We can talk over dinner later. You'll still have dinner with me? I haven't put you off?"

"Of course. I said I would, and nothing has changed my mind."

"Excellent."

"I do look forward to another evening in your company." Emma hoped her feelings were obvious.

"So formal."

"For now."

Maggie put her hand in her jacket pocket and frowned. "Where's the key?" She patted her other pockets.

"The kitchen door key?" Emma asked. "You left that for me this morning."

Maggie smiled. "I did, didn't I. There's no need to wait outside for me, then. Let yourself in and make yourself at home. You know where your room is?"

My room? Emma wondered at the mention of the guest room. "Thank you. Do you often give the key to your house to anyone you meet?"

"Only the attractive ones." Maggie winked. "But don't use all the hot water. After a few hours at the farm, I stink and need all the hot water I can get."

Emma laughed. "All right. I'll save you some."

"It's a date."

"It is."

15

SHOPPING

E mma opened the front door and dragged several bags of rubbish outside. With no place else to dump them, she abandoned the bags of trash on the weed-covered front garden. This was only the first day of cleaning; there would be many more to come.

As she dropped off the bags, she noted the curtains twitching in several of the windows nearby.

"Nosey buggers," she murmured to herself. It was amusing the first few times she'd seen it—she'd never considered herself to be worthy of such attention—but now it wasn't funny anymore.

She marched back inside the house and slammed the door closed behind her.

"Enough," she grumbled. In the kitchen, she removed her bright yellow marigolds and threw the rubber gloves into the sink. Then she draped her apron over a kitchen chair. She wondered, for about three seconds, whether she should change into something more presentable, but decided not to bother. If they wanted to take a good look at her, then they could do so in all her messy, dirty glory.

She grabbed her handbag and left the house. She didn't

even bother locking the door; with such attention from her neighbors, no burglars would dare to try and get inside her house. Her things, mostly clothes and cleaning products, were safe enough, and anyone who took them obviously needed them more than she did.

She marched along the street, her back ramrod straight and her chin up. She had no idea where she was going, but headed along the nearest side street. It was about time she took a look at the neighborhood.

She found Market Street tucked away at the back end of town. It was out of sight of the main road and so avoided most traffic. She stopped as she realized, for the first time, how little traffic noise she could hear. In fact, the only consistent sounds came from the birds, and there were so many of them and they were a noisy bunch.

A tractor engine rumbled in the distance, and she heard the growls of land rovers and a few cars, but little else. She couldn't hear any loud music, or any residents screaming at each other. She couldn't hear the sound of the underground trains, or the sirens of the emergency vehicles. She shivered. The lack of noise was strange when only the night before she'd complained how noisy the whole place had been in the storm.

Farther along, she came across the shops. Unlike the glass and shiny commercial spaces in town, these shops were little more than converted houses. With each house built from local stone rather than red brick, they all blended together in a quaint and attractive way. At the same time, the shops offered everything anyone could want. A butcher supplied meat and fish, and a baker made bread and a small selection of cakes. A small hardware store had enough to get anyone out of trouble, and a small supermarket sold pretty much everything else, including wine. That alone warranted a visit.

Ahead stood the church, with its steeple amongst the trees. On the other side of the road, she noted a café with a small table and two chairs outside. It looked busy inside, which always boded well. At the crossroads, the corner building looked no different from any house, except that above the door a small sign swung with a gentle creak in the afternoon breeze. The door was ajar; the Castlecoombe Inn was open for business, and Emma was more than a little tempted to indulge in a large gin and tonic or two. Instead, she went to the supermarket.

An old crone sat behind the counter watching daytime television on a tiny set as she talked with a silver-haired woman. They were chatting away, their voices loud and their conversation energetic. Until Emma stepped through the door.

Voices on the television laughed, but in the sudden silence of the store, the canned laughter sounded hollow and false. Their eyes followed her as she walked the aisles, but Emma was getting used to people looking at her. She ignored them and hummed the flower duet from the opera *Lakme*. The volume of the television dropped to the point where Emma's humming seemed loud. She carried on; they could all do with a little culture.

Into her basket, she dropped a small carton of milk, a packet of crackers, a small slab of mature cheddar, a smaller wedge of Stilton, and most important of all, a couple bottles of wine. The choices were not brilliant, but she'd seen worse.

"Hello," she said, with as much cheer as she could muster.

"Hello. Passing through, are you?" the shopkeeper asked.

"Not at all," she said with her exaggerated cheeriness. "I've moved in. Well, kind of."

"The Tapper house, isn't it?" the other woman chimed in.

"Yes, it is," Emma said, turning to the other customer. "You must have seen me arrive last night."

"Aye," she said. "I did. And who you be?"

Blunt, Emma thought to herself. "I'm Maud Tapper's

niece." As the words came out of her mouth, the air turned frosty.

The shopkeeper stared at her over the rims of her glasses. "Well, Tapper, I hope you're not here to cause our Lord Magwood no harm. If you have mischief in your heart, leave now."

"The Lord who?" Emma asked, confused.

"Aye, Lord Magwood Durrant you would say, from the Hall up the hill."

"Oh yes, I see. Maggie you mean."

"That would be Lord Durrant to the likes of you."

"It's all right. She, the Lord Durrant, that is, asked me to call her Maggie."

The shopkeeper almost choked. "Too kind for her own good, that one, and she takes good care of the estate and the people on it. Not like the brother. I'm surprised she don't give up, or go mad. And with her family misfortunes, it makes her very special. But you already know this, being a Tapper and all."

"Know what?"

"Shush," the other woman interrupted, and her eyes hardened in warning.

"You and your curses, child. Do you not feel guilty at the harm you have piled upon the poor girl, and her father, too?"

"What are you talking about?" Emma asked, intrigued.

"Come to gloat, I bet," the other shopper chipped in without answering. "You should be ashamed."

"Curses? Gloat? I have no idea what you're talking about. I like Maggie. I think she's a wonderful and genuine woman. In fact, we're having dinner later. No mischief in dinner, is there?"

The two women looked at each other, and a whole world of unspoken meaning passed between them. If Emma had thought the air turned chilly when she said she was a Tapper, then the atmosphere turned positively arctic at the mention of dinner.

"That'll be eighteen pounds and twenty-seven pence." The storekeeper's eyes narrowed. "If you're taking this wine for Lord Magwood to drink, then she won't like it much. She prefers this." She pulled a bottle from under the counter and placed it where Emma could see. "This is her favorite."

"I see," Emma said. "Then I'll put one of these back and take one of those."

"Very well," she said, her eyes shining. "Make it twenty-five pounds twenty-six pence."

"And a carrier bag."

"Twenty-five pounds and thirty-six pence," the woman said. She grabbed a plastic bag from under the counter and dropped it next to Emma's purchases. "Thanks for stopping by, Tapper."

Somewhat nonplussed, Emma wandered along the street with her few items of shopping. She didn't really think about where she was headed; her thoughts raced too much. As she walked farther from the shops, the houses grew farther apart. Close to the shops they had been tight little terraces, and then they grew to a few semi-detached cottages, and then the larger houses that stood farther apart from each other.

At the end of the road, the lych-gate marked the way to the to the churchyard and cemetery. The gate swayed in the wind and the hinges creaked a warning. Or was it an invitation to enter? Emma would have turned around, but there was a single Land Rover outside the gates, and she recognized it from the courtyard at the hall.

Maggie? she wondered, but there was no one in sight. For a moment, and it was so brief it almost didn't qualify as a moment at all, Emma toyed with the idea of turning around and going straight back to the cottage, but she was here now. Her curiosity grew. Why was Maggie here? And then another thought struck her. Would she be able to find the graves of her family? Were they interred here?

The small church, with a tall steeple at the other end, sat in a large plot, surrounded by old, crumbling tombstones and grave markers. To the right of the church, a small iron gate formed a passage through a thick hedge. Emma took a step further into the cemetery and peered through the greenery. Beyond the gate, in a small enclosure surrounded by yet more privet, lay row upon row of modern graves. To the left of the church stood a high wall that was crumbling with age. A small wooden gate permitted a view of older and darker tombstones.

Old graves were always more interesting, Emma thought, so she turned to the left. There, weeping angels looked down on worn stone markers, and crosses, eroded by wind and time, pointed in every direction except up.

In the far corner of this private graveyard, Maggie knelt and placed white roses against a headstone. Emma watched her for a while, although her gaze wandered across the lives and deaths of the people of the village. Her eyes snapped back to Maggie when she stood up, walked to another grave, and placed red roses against that headstone. She repeated these actions, putting red roses at several graves and white roses at several more, in some kind of pattern or ritual that Emma could not discern from where she stood.

Before Maggie could run out of roses, Emma found her way to the modern section. Now was not the time to intrude on Maggie's grief. Besides, she didn't want Maggie to think the new Tapper was stalking her.

Curiosity, though, wouldn't let her forget. She lost herself in names again, and when she heard the roar of a diesel engine, she wandered back to the front of the church to see the Land Rover and Maggie departing.

She was alone with the dead, and her curiosity again

arose. She had to know what Maggie was doing, and she had a shrewd idea of where she had been.

Emma stepped through the wall into the small enclosure and headed toward the rose-covered graves. Two in particular stood out more than the others.

A neat, scripted headstone, covered with six red roses, marked the resting place of Maggie's father and mother. Her father had died young, aged thirty, and some years later, his wife joined him with a heart broken from losing him. They left behind a young daughter and a son.

"Oh, Maggie," she whispered.

Yet the grave with the most flowers stood almost hidden in the corner of the churchyard. A dozen pure white roses, in a small stone vase, stood bright against the green hedge and the small, weathered headstone.

Emily Tapper. Departed this life, aged sixteen
in the year of our Lord 1643.
Beloved daughter of John and Mary Tapper

Emma read the headstone several times. This was where it all started. She knelt by the grave, her thoughts in turmoil.

"Hello, grandmother several times removed," she said. "I don't know if I need to say how many greats there are, but if you were here right now, I would call you grandmother." She ran her hand over the rough stone, pitted by age and weather, and smiled to herself. "Hello, grandmother. I'm back now. I'm home."

16

WEASEL

Weasel was not one to take the direct route anywhere. Some might say he was the sort who simply couldn't follow the expected path even if he tried. Some might say his attention was constantly split by things he found along the way, such as an opportunity for personal gain. Some would say he wasn't smart enough to figure out the direct route even if he wanted to. And some might say his purpose was to obscure actions that were less than virtuous. There was truth in all of those speculations, some more than others.

Weasel prided himself on being a professional—anything less and he would be headed straight back into a cell. This job sounded easy enough, though. That Charles fella had given him all the details he needed. It was simple: Go in, deal with the girl, and help himself. He could shift silver easy enough; he knew a man in the city. Chaps like him always knew a man in the city. He chuckled to himself. Charles had suggested one of the pawnbrokers. Idiot. Still. It would be a good payoff, and he would have himself a little fun, too. He'd wanted to suss out the house first, but he was pushed for time. As long as he took care, and he always took every precaution—well, as much as he could—then he would be all right.

Magwood Hall was a little too isolated, and the village equally so, to remain anonymous. If he took his car and parked it on a street nearby, someone would notice. Instead, he preferred a more circuitous route.

He walked to the local train station with a rucksack filled with all the equipment he might need. He'd included a tarp, bin bags, torch, nitrile surgical gloves—he was allergic to latex—a knife, screwdrivers, an Allen key set, and a set of lockpicks. At the station, he bought a ticket to the city, paid with cash, and made sure he wasn't seen on the CCTV cameras. He wore a hooded jacket in case he missed any cameras, and tight leather gloves.

He took the next slow train, the one that stopped at every station until the end of the line, and got on board. At the next station, he disembarked. It was a small station, and they didn't have cameras. There, he slipped onto a side street and checked that no one had installed new cameras since his last visit. There, he helped himself to a beaten-up old Ford. It didn't take long.

Weasel put his coat on the passenger seat, along with his backpack, and covered the front seat with a single piece of thin plastic sheeting. It was awkward to control the thin plastic with gloves on, but he managed. Finally, he was ready.

He drove through the mountains toward Castlecoombe, but took a narrow road around the north side of the Inger. At the far side of the Castlecoombe valley, he turned onto a disused logger's service road and, at the end, parked up in a small lay-by, hidden amidst trees and bushes. It was a great place to leave the car. The area was used by dog walkers and mountain walkers, and no one would care at all about one more fell walker parking in the middle of nowhere.

He waited for a while in case anyone else pulled up, but no one did. It was almost lunchtime and a little late in the day for serious walkers to make a start but too early for them to turn back. The more he looked around the spot, the more he approved. The gravel would hide his footprints, and although there had been a lot of heavy rain of late, the ground had already started to dry out. If anything, the bright sun made the whole walk very pleasant.

Even though Weasel wore gloves, he grabbed antibacterial wipes from his backpack. He didn't go for any particular type as a rule, but these were branded and on special offer. After all, a bargain was a bargain, and Weasel never could resist a bargain. He wiped down everything he had touched, including the seats, the gear stick, the steering wheel, the dashboard, and the doors. By the time he finished, the car was cleaner than it had been when he'd pinched it. He was a cautious fellow; the last thing he needed was to be arrested for stealing a car, not with his history.

With luck, it would still be waiting for him when he finished. If not, he'd just steal another one.

He slung his old kit bag over his shoulder and strode down a trail heading, at least at first, in the wrong direction. He would slip round the hill when he felt safe and not before.

Contrary to expectations, Magwood Hall was a hive of activity. Cleaners and housekeepers were everywhere, and when they started to disappear, burly men with maintenance overalls appeared. A team of window cleaners climbed all over the place, and Weasel saw so many other workers, he wondered if anyone would notice if he drove right up to one of the garages. That would be pushing his luck, though, and a thief, a careful thief, never pushed his luck.

He'd chosen to arrive early so he could get a good look at the place. He also wanted to check the information he had been given because one thing he knew was to never rely on anyone else. He found himself a nice spot at the edge of the woods a little above Magwood Hall. It was far enough away that with care, no one would notice him, but close enough that he could see and listen to people come and go. A grassy hillock would hide him well and yet provided a view to watch. Perfect. He settled in and watched the comings and goings of the tradespeople and, he assumed, people who worked there.

Weasel despaired at the number of people. Charles said it would be quiet, but it wasn't.

"You're a fool, Charles. You know squat about your own home."

Then he concerned himself with looking about for the sister. He watched for a while, but soon got bored.

He found a nice comfortable place in the long grass, laid down a small tarpaulin from his backpack, and settled in to wait. The sun was warm for a change, and the area was quiet. He lay back, cleaned his nails with the tip of a small pocketknife, and listened to the cars come and go.

His mind wandered; his thoughts filled with the valuables he would find. Gold, silver, maybe some jewelry, and then, well, he could not forget his other promise.

Waiting was hard work, but thinking of her, the Lady Lord, kept his mind busy. He imagined what she was like: not too tall, slim, elegant, a bit like her brother. He didn't care too much what she looked like. Fair hair and female was more than enough, and according to Charles, all she needed was a good man. Weasel reckoned he was such a man, and with such thoughts filling his mind, a quickening inside his trousers agreed with him.

She deserved it. They all did. That was in his file, too. But this one deserved it even more. After all, she was the one stopping him from getting the money he was due from her brother. If Charles had paid up on time, then Weasel wouldn't be in trouble with the boss, who wanted his balls on a plate for slow collection of outstanding debt. He'd avoided trouble only by promising a share of his take. One way or another, he and his boss would be paid, and it would be today.

Weasel sneered and hissed with irritation. Anger did not make the bulge diminish. It never did. But this time there was the chance of satisfaction, and he liked that idea. He liked the sheer expansiveness of unlimited reparation quite a lot. She would pay, without doubt. All he had to do was to decide what ways she would pay and how often. He decided she would be soft of body after all, she didn't do any real work. She spent her time lording it over everyone, including her brother. It was not right a woman should have control. She would be pliable, ready, and he relished the thought of her softness underneath him, enveloping him. Afterward, she would beg for more, as any woman would.

He slipped his hand inside his jeans, and as he thought of all the things he would do, he massaged himself to a swift end and wiped himself off with an old rag from his pocket. He lay back and stared up at the blue sky. He was a contented man, and his broad grin split his face so wide even the crows overhead could see the stained stubs he called his teeth. Life was good, he thought, and it was going to get better.

Weasel woke up some hours later. The westering sun cast the side of the hill into gloom, and the loss of the sun chilled him to wakefulness. He stretched and yawned before he looked at Magwood Hall once more.

All the cars and vans had disappeared, as he'd expected, except for a small red car. That confused him for moment. He didn't know anyone in the village who had such an inappropriate vehicle, and he was sure it hadn't been there when he first arrived. Weasel shook his head and almost laughed. He had fixed the Land Rover good and proper after all. Perhaps it was a total wreck, and this pathetic little shopping cart-sized thing was the only rental she could get. The idea of some fancy lord diminished to a tiny city car amused him to no end. The day was getting better and better.

Weasel checked his watch. He looked at the sky, too. It was time to make a move. He put everything into his bag and slung it over his shoulders. He covered his head and face with a ski mask and pulled on a pair of purple nitrile gloves. They were better than his others, but walking around town with purple gloves would draw attention.

He looked at the main building, his eyes darting from window to window, but there was no sign of activity. Weasel scrambled the rest of the way from the woods to the back of the barn and crossed the gravel path to the nearest wall of the house. He didn't make a sound.

Adrenalin surged and his heart pounded. He loved his job.

He inched his way along the side of the building, ignoring the large front door, and headed to the smaller one that, according to Charles, went into the kitchen. The front door would be locked; the kitchen, he'd suggested, probably wouldn't be.

Weasel stopped near the door and positioned himself to one side so his shadow couldn't be seen from within. Then he listened.

It was quiet, very quiet.

The handle to the kitchen door turned in his grip, and he didn't make a sound. That was a good sign. He could feel the latch retract, and he opened the door a fraction and listened carefully.

17

INSIDE

The kitchen seemed quiet. Not silent, of course. He heard sounds that faded into the steady regularity of background noise. The clicking of a clock, the hum of a fridge and possibly a freezer, he thought. Most important of all, he couldn't hear any sounds of people within.

He pushed the door open a little further and peered inside. The door led to a short passage, or antechamber. Boots lined the wall, and Weasel noted, with some satisfaction, all of the spaces on the rack were filled with clean and dry footwear. With no signs of dirt under the rack, he was sure no one had come in from the farm whilst he'd been sleeping. The floor, all clean quarry tiles, also showed no sign of recent passage. This was good, too. He pushed the door open further, and it shifted with the barest squeak.

He paused one last time and, when he couldn't detect anything untoward, stepped into the antechamber and closed the back door behind him.

Weasel stopped at the threshold of the kitchen, and when he compared the space with his single hotplate and a microwave in the corner of his one-room bed-sit, he almost whistled. Also, unlike any kitchen he'd ever seen, this one wasn't square. It was more L-shaped with some niches, which was why there were more corners than he expected.

His gaze swept across the rooms, and when he saw nothing that might be threatening, he took a tentative step forward. On the floor, the flagstone slabs were perfect for a quiet entry. This pleased Weasel. It was so easy.

Even though he considered himself an expert at illicit entries, his heart beat a little faster. He recognized the fear mixed with anticipation. It kept his mind alert and focussed on the job at hand. The thrill of being some place he should not was as exciting as the fear and the anticipation. It was all good.

He stole through the empty kitchen, every step placed with quiet care, just in case one of the stones had come loose. First, he took in the layout of the kitchen, the ways around the room, any hazards should he need to exit with great speed, and the doors. Other than the door to the outside, there were two doors left ajar at the other end of the kitchen and another closed door almost hidden behind a pillar beside the windows.

It's like a museum, he thought. Like one of those posh houses he'd been to as a kid. Now he was back again to rob one. Like those other houses, here the floors had been cleaned and were free of obstruction. Wooden shelves and cabinets lined the walls. They were nicked and marked, yet polished to a light-reflecting shine. A large range churned out heat and kept the kitchen warm, and on the far side of the room, the two doorways opened into wide corridors, also with stone-flagged floor.

Weasel smirked to himself. It was so easy to sneak; almost too easy. He inched around the side of the room. With each step, he mapped his escape route or hiding place should it become necessary. He was as prepared as he could be.

A whisper caught his attention before he reached the doorway on the other side of the room, and he froze. Instinct had him closing his eyes, and his other senses stretched outward. The hum of the fluorescent lights filled the air, the solid and mechanical chunking of the clock punctuated the hiss of the fridge, and quietest of all, the gentle *blup-blup* of something bubbling. His eyes flew open and he turned, without thought, toward the pan of water coming to boil on the range. A teapot and a cup and saucer sat on the side table.

"Shit," he breathed. He'd not heard the water, nor had he looked for it. She, the Lord high and mighty, would be back for her tea.

He heard footsteps. Close. *Click-clack, clickity-clack*. The sound of solid heels on stone.

A whisper echoed through the room, *"Do you…"*

A cold fist of panic took hold of his innards and squeezed. The clock ticked, and as the adrenaline flowed, his senses sharpened. Small sounds seemed far too loud. Details caught his attention. Colors washed out to a stark monotone. Even the edges of the table appeared sharper.

Tick…

The world slowed. The bubbling in the pan calmed to a gentle *blup.* He turned his head with exaggerated slowness, and although his mind seemed to work at normal speed, the rest of his body did not.

…Tock.

The pan continued to boil in slow motion. *Blup.*

One glance, and he measured how long it would take to get to the back door and whether he could do it unseen. He couldn't. The distance was too great and in his estimation the person would appear at the door any second. *Click-clack, clickity-clack*, as the footsteps drew closer.

Tick…

The door by the windows, half opened, caught his attention. It was only a few steps away, but he didn't recall the door being open. A cool draft from the darkness on the other side of the doorway reminded him of outside. Maybe the breeze had pushed it open. The details didn't matter; it was dark and unlikely that anyone was there. More important, it was a way out.

Weasel dashed through the opening, but no matter how fast he tried to move, his feet dragged as though he raced through sludge. Then, when he thought he would never make it, he slipped through the doorway. Just in time.

…Tock.

Cool became dark and dank. He chilled so fast goosebumps covered his arms. Narrow wooden steps creaked under his weight, and a smell of musty dampness wafted from below. He took a step down, and cold stone brushed against his arm. He moved his backpack over one shoulder. There was not enough room to turn around with it on his back.

Tick. Tock.

He heard the clock as he stepped down onto the wooden landing. The press of the dark surrounded him as he shut the door, silently, carefully. He took a deep, lungful of breath, and relief flooded through him.

"Damn it," he whispered, confident no one could hear him through the door. But what if the door had been open because someone had come down here first? "Fuck!"

Through the door he heard footsteps, and the *click-clack, clickity-clack* grew closer.

Fuck. The steps were heading toward him. He had to go further down. Maybe the stairwell had a basement he could hide in.

He turned around on the narrow step, and his pack scraped across the wall. Fool. There were no lights on. He waited for his eyes to adjust. Dim light seeped into the stairwell from around the door. The thin beams of light picked out motes of dust that danced like a flurry of snow. He swept his hand along the one wall and hoped he could find a light pull. There wasn't one. He tried the other side but didn't find anything

Darkness it was, then.

Weasel looked down at his feet. He stood on a small landing, and steps did lead further down. In this light, though, he could see no farther than the first step. He stood on the edge of an abyss. Fear, the primal fear of the dark, wrenched his insides, and beads of perspiration broke along his brow. He stretched out a hand and leaned on the cool rock.

"Do you?" he heard from a great distance, and then all was quiet.

Weasel reached into his pocket and pulled out a small penlight. Relief that he'd found it made him giddy.

He shone the light down the steps. It wasn't a very bright torch, but dim light was usually all he needed. Something that lit up the whole area and called attention to his presence was not a good thing.

"Much better," he mumbled, for no other reason than to help settle his nerves. He was in control now that he had light, except for being so scared. "Jesus," he hissed, "scared of shadows now." But he had light, and he'd already started to weave this into a funny story for his mates down at the pub. He grinned instead.

"Do you?" a voice screamed into his left ear. *"DO. YOU?"*

"What the fuck!" He spun around so fast he grazed his shoulder against the wall. Out of the blackness, a white face from his worst nightmare appeared in front of him. She had white skin, an open mouth, green lips, and a swollen black tongue that protruded from the corner of her mouth. He almost screamed, but something slithered around his throat and tightened.

He struggled for breath, each constricted rasp allowing him less and less air, until his lungs turned to fire. The force around his neck snapped him upwards, pulled him onto his toes. Weasel struggled. Struggled for breath, struggled to live, struggled so hard he missed the step and fell face forward down the steps. *Thunk.* His face hit the first step and went numb. *Thunk.* Onto the second step, but now his face seemed to bounce, as though made of rubber. *Thunk. Thunk.* After the third or fourth step, he didn't feel a thing. Not even when his backpack split open and his knife, the one still bearing the signs of blood left from his last victim, spilled from the bag and landed almost within reach of his hand.

"Mine," said a distant voice. *"She is mine."*

"**M**aggie? Is that you?" Emma called out as she made her way down the stairs.

She heard no reply.

She shrugged. She thought she'd heard footsteps but decided she must have imagined it. The house was so big that there were creaks and groans everywhere. She noted the pan of boiling water and removed it from the stove to make herself a cup of tea. She wished Maggie would come home; the house felt empty without her. Spooky, too. She sighed, and the house seemed to sigh with her.

Upstairs, she made herself comfortable in the bathroom. A huge bathtub, water almost to the top, her mug of tea on a table to the side, along with a book she'd been promising to read for years.

"What luxury," she crooned, as she dumped her clothes on a chair and lowered herself into the scented, bubble-covered hot water. Pity there was no one here to scrub her back. She smiled at the thought and let the water soak away every tight muscle in her body.

18

MAGGIE IN THE KITCHEN

Maggie parked her Land Rover close to the kitchen door and whistled as she unloaded bags of groceries onto the back step. She checked the door and was pleased to find it unlocked. It would certainly look odd if she had to ring the doorbell to her own house.

Inside the kitchen, she looked around and was disappointed Emma wasn't in the kitchen waiting for her. How arrogant she was! She chided herself for her thoughts and set about bringing the rest of the shopping into the house.

Inside the fridge, she found a bottle of wine on the middle shelf. She touched the bottle, already chilled and begging to be opened. She also noticed a bottle of *Saint Emillion* on the kitchen table with a note that read, "I didn't know what you had planned so I got red and white."

She couldn't help but smile, but it froze on her face when she spotted the open cellar door.

Why was it open? She looked inside the dark stairwell, but the lights were off. "Anyone there?"

No one answered her.

For a moment, she feared Emma had wandered into the cellar, and a cold block of ice washed through her chest and settled like an iceberg in her belly. The steps weren't safe, so she hadn't used the cellar in years. That's why the door was supposed to be locked. "Please, no." Her heart thudded against her ribs.

She reached around the door frame and pulled a length of string weighed down with a ceramic toggle. The light, a small, low-wattage bulb, swung from the ceiling. "Emma?" No answer, and then the light pinged and went out. "Damn."

Maggie shuffled through one of the drawers looking for either a bulb or a torch. The bathroom pipework banged and clanged, and water whooshed along the pipes. The bathroom pipes made that noise when they were used. She'd always intended to get that fixed, but right then, she couldn't have been happier. Emma was upstairs. Unless it was Charles? She shook her head; his car wasn't outside. It had to be her.

Relief turned her knees to jelly. She closed the cellar door and leaned against it. "You're safe," she whispered. Emma was upstairs. Nevertheless, she locked the cellar door and put the key on the hook nearby. Just to make sure the door wouldn't open, she shook the handle and tried to open it. The door remained closed and locked.

The urge to go to Emma and make sure that she was all right almost overwhelmed her. But Emma had been in the bathroom. She'd not be ready for guests. She probably wouldn't be dressed.

"Stop it!" she chided herself. She had to do something useful, like finish putting the shopping away. She had a great many things to do if she was to cook dinner.

She whistled the melody to something she'd heard on the radio as she chopped vegetables and put them in a crockpot. Her hand stopped halfway between chopping board and pot as a chill wind blew across the back of her neck. She waited for the clock to mark the lengthening of time. But it sounded pretty normal.

Tick. Tock.

Tick. Tock.

Tick…

In the distance she heard the *click-clack, clickity-clack* of shoes on stone. A voice echoed from afar, the words as yet too indistinct to understand.

…Tock.

Maggie paused. Her fingers gripped the knife handle, and she readied herself to react.

Tick…

The knife was ripped from her grasp, hit the table, and stood on end, with its handle in the air. The knife pirouetted about the tip and gouged into the wood.

"Don't be childish," Maggie admonished. "And leave us alone."

…Tock.

Various implements—a ladle, a set of tongs, two spatulas, and a whisk— disengaged themselves from their racks around the kitchen and hung, motionless, in the air.

Tick…

One by one, each item flew across the room. A procession of knives rose from the knife block and flew at the cellar door. The sound of the blades embedding into the wood echoed through the kitchen. Other less pointed objects flew at Maggie, then dropped to the wooden tabletop and marched around like something from *The Sorcerer's Apprentice.*

…Tock.

"Stop it! I'm trying to cook." Everything stopped. The implements stood on their tips and leaned away as though listening to her.

"Look, I know you hate me, know you will orchestrate my death. I'm ready, but not yet, huh?" She snickered to herself. Only a Durrant firstborn would be talking to kitchen utensils. "I have a guest. She's the Tapper heir, and she deserves a good meal, at least. So behave and let me feed her in safety." She smiled. "I like her. Don't scare her off. She's upstairs getting ready. I bet she's used all the hot water already."

Tick...

"Dooooo youuu..."

"I don't know," Maggie answered. "I honestly don't know."

Cold silence, thick with the touch of the otherworld, filled the kitchen.

"Do you?"

...Tock.

The sense of her visitor vanished and time resumed as usual. All the implements dancing about her table fell over and clattered on the wood. Once more, the normal sounds of the kitchen filled her ears and she was alone again.

Tick. Tock. The clock announced the passing seconds with mechanical precision.

Maggie leaned on the table to catch her breath. She held her hand out and it shook. This encounter was a little more direct than usual, and increasing directness was a concern. She helped herself to a large tot of cooking brandy to settle her nerves. It was hard to prepare dinner when any moment might be her last.

In her mind, she could still hear the knives as they thudded, one by one, into the wooden cellar door.

She needed a break, but she had things to do first. Foremost would be putting the knives and utensils back where they belonged.

It took a great deal of willpower and mental fortitude to continue food preparation and cooking. She forced her trembling hands to chop meat and vegetables and add them to a large oval casserole dish that had been in the family for generations. Her grandmother had called it her crockpot, and when done she settled the lid on top and popped the lot into the oven.

She washed her hand in the sunken Belfast sink, and when

she was done, gripped the cold ceramic edges with both hands.

"Now," she said, "I'm going to get cleaned up for dinner, and it would be nice if the carpets don't move when I walk across them, with no flashing lights. I would like to avoid strangulation as well, if you don't mind. I quite like breathing. All in all, it would be marvelous if you didn't try to kill me in front of Emma…Emma Tapper, that is. Deal?"

No one answered.

"No matter," she said aloud. "I have a better idea." She opened the chilled white wine, half-filled two glasses, and put them on a tray. "Let's see if Emma fancies a glass before dinner, shall we?"

Maggie made it all the way upstairs without mishap and stood at Emma's door with her hand raised, poised to knock.

Was she being too forward?

She shook her head. Life was too short to worry, and she expected hers to be shorter than most. She rapped on the wooden door with a degree of confidence she did not feel and waited.

Emma opened the door wearing nothing more than a dressing gown. "Maggie…"

It took a moment for the heir of Durrant to speak. "I…er… brought wine. I thought it would be nice before dinner."

Emma looked thoughtful, and then she grinned. "My, Lord Magwood…" She curtsied, but it looked awkward and strange as she used both hands to stop the dressing gown from falling open.

The thought of Emma wearing nothing more than a dressing gown got her flustered. It covered Emma from mid-thigh up, but flashes of pale skin, close but not close enough, sent more than her heart rate to pounding levels.

Maggie blushed. "What? What's that in aid of? Why?"

Emma wrapped her gown about her body. "That's who you are."

"No. Yes, but no one calls me Magwood."

"Everyone calls you Magwood." She smiled.

Maggie searched for something to say, but nothing came to mind.

"They don't seem so keen to see *me*, though, being a Tapper and all," Emma added. "Now, don't just stand there, Maggie You'll spill my wine, and I don't want you to waste any of it."

"Well."

"And when you come in here, you can sit down and tell me all the things you haven't mentioned yet."

"All of them?" she managed.

"Yes. All of them."

Maggie drew her brows together and frowned. "You're right, Emma. Things are not straightforward."

"You sound so serious."

"I think I need more wine," she said.

"Come inside and talk to me."

Maggie stared into Emma's eyes. "I better not. I have things to do before dinner."

"Are you trying to escape me?"

Maggie dragged her eyes away and stared down the corridor. "I think you need to get dressed, and then we'll talk."

"Dressed?" Emma echoed.

"Yes, please. Then come down when you're ready, and we'll talk as I cook. We'll eat in the kitchen if you don't mind. It's cozier."

"Perfect," she answered.

19

DINNER

Maggie stood in the kitchen and stared at the cellar door. She hadn't notice it at first, but the moment she'd approached the range, she couldn't miss either the open door, or the chill wind that blew from the dark depths. More scratches had been added to the knife points made earlier, and the coffin-shaped design sent a shiver down her spine. Pointillism by knife was a new addition to the madness of the house. She hoped it didn't spread to other doors or other rooms.

"Hi, Maggie, what's up?" Emma asked.

Maggie flinched; she'd not heard her come into the kitchen. She turned around and smiled briefly. "Did you open this door?"

"No. Why would I?"

"That's what I thought." Maggie scratched the top of her head. "No one should be down there, so the door shouldn't be open."

"I wouldn't go around looking in places I have no right to be, you know."

"Sorry, that's not what I meant. You can go wherever you please. It's just that this leads to the cellars."

"Where the wine is?"

Now Maggie chuckled. "No, it's been abandoned for years. The steps are dangerous at the best of times, but some are rotted and others are missing. It's not safe, so I keep the door locked usually."

Maggie closed the door with more force than needed, and the it *thunked* into place. As she locked the door–again–the door sighed.

"Maybe there's a draft?" Emma suggested.

"A draft with the power to open a locked door?"

Emma shrugged. "Are you positive you–"

"Yes," Maggie interrupted. Although, the door *was* open and the key was still on the hook on the wall next to the door. It wasn't Emma's fault that she didn't understand this house or her life. She closed her eyes and took a deep breath. "I'm sorry, that was rude of me."

"It's all right."

"No. It isn't all right. There is no excuse for rudeness."

"It's fine, honest."

"Anyway, it occurs to me that at the other end of the cellar there is a drop chute for coal. Perhaps the cover's broken and the draft comes from there."

"There you go."

"I'll take a look down the cellar tomorrow." She frowned. "Nothing I can do right now anyway."

"Meanwhile, there are more important things to worry about," Emma said.

"What things would they be?"

"This," Emma waved her empty glass about. "There seems to be a high degree of evaporation in this kitchen."

Maggie laughed and picked up her own empty glass. "Look at this, my glass also has an evaporation problem."

"It's a damned nuisance, if you ask me."

"We'd better do something about it. Red or white?"

"Depends on what we're eating, I suppose."

"Does it matter?"

"Not really, no. But sometimes different things need different wines, and you being a lord and all, I'd better be on my best behavior."

"Don't."

"Don't what?"

"Please don't do things to please me. Be yourself. Being you will please me most of all."

Emma paused. "All right, I will. I think I'll stick to the white for the moment."

Maggie filled each glass with a good measure. "Better?"

Emma nodded. "So then, you are my Lord Magwood."

Maggie rolled her eyes. "I know, I know. But you knew that."

"I know you as Lord Maggie Durrant. Which is right?"

"Both." She served dinner before she said more. "My father wanted to call me Charles."

"A girl called Charles? You could have been called Charlie. That's a girl's name, isn't it?"

"No to Charlie, it had to be Charles. He was so angry at my mother for giving him a daughter when he wanted a son."

"But it's not her fault."

"I know, I know. Male pride, I suppose, but my mother wouldn't have it, and they had this huge argument. To assert his authority, he insisted I be called Magwood. I think it's a great name. When I went to school, instead of being teased, they thought it was different and interesting. Being different was quite the thing, so I fell in with a good crowd, and they shortened it to Maggie. The name has stuck ever since."

"What happened to your parents?" Emma asked. She didn't want Maggie to know she had seen her at the cemetery.

Maggie stared at her for a moment. "Dead," she answered.

"I'm so sorry, Maggie."

"It's all right. It happened a long time ago."

"Do you want to talk about it?"

Maggie shrugged. "My father died when I was a child, and my mother never got over his death. She hung on until I was sixteen and then gave up on life."

"I'm sorry," Emma repeated. "I shouldn't pry."

"Why not? I would."

"And you have a brother?"

"Charles Stephen."

"I haven't seen him yet."

"No. He's off about town, lording it up."

Emma quirked one eyebrow. "And 'lording it up' involves what, exactly?"

"Getting drunk, I suppose. Getting a woman for the night. He's very proud of such things."

"Men often are."

Maggie laughed, and the guilt of even mentioning her brother lessened.

"Did you know the people in the town are very protective of you? They think you're some kind of angel and I'm some sort of scarlet woman, or something, come to bring you down."

Maggie almost choked on her food.

"So you agree? Is that what I am?"

"Not at all. As you know, there's a bit of a history between your family and mine. Country memory is like the land; it lasts for a long time. And in their eyes, you've committed a cardinal sin."

"What sin is that?" Emma asked.

"You weren't born in the village, so they distrust you."

"Right. I understand. I think."

"They'll grow to like you eventually."

"If I stay?"

Maggie didn't answer that.

"Which leads me to another question. Why were you waiting for me at the gatehouse?"

Maggie deliberated on her answer. On the one hand, she had promised to tell Emma everything, but on the other, how well did she know this woman? After all, she was a Tapper, no matter everything else.

"I was expecting you to arrive at some point, and I was nosey."

"You said as much already, but it's not much of an answer, is it?" Emma rested her hand on Maggie's. "Is it?"

"I suppose not," Maggie conceded.

"There's something going on, but I don't know what. And you're reluctant to speak of it. But I don't want to ruin such a super evening."

Maggie looked at their touching hands. What could she say to that?

Emma pulled her hand back. "Anyway, it's none of my business. I'm the stranger here, after all."

"It's not like that, Emma."

"But it is, isn't it? I'm the outsider in a small distrustful village. I wonder how long it will be before you trust me?"

"Emma, please, don't say it like that. It's complicated."

"Of course, it is. I know it would take a long time for the village to trust me, even if I stayed."

"Will you? Stay in Castlecoombe?"

"Truthfully? I don't know. I haven't yet seen what it is like to live here, and while staying with you is very pleasant, it's not the same as living here. I thought I would get my house set up and move in whilst I decided what to do. I have to get it ready for sale anyway."

"But it's not ready for you!"

Emma grinned. "I've tidied up quite a lot. I should concentrate on getting the rest of it done. When I was cleaning upstairs, I found that one of the mattresses is new and wrapped in plastic. Once I work out how to do the fire and get some wood in, I think I'll be quite cozy."

Maggie looked thoughtful. "Are you not happy here, in this house?"

"It's not about being happy, Maggie. I need to get settled here, and I've imposed on your generosity more than I should."

"You don't have to go, you know."

"I think I must."

Maggie didn't want to hear that. "If it makes you happy."

Emma nodded.

"Then I'll do what I can to assist."

"Thank you. I would appreciate your help. You can show me how to light the fire, for a start."

Maggie laughed, and the escalating tension vanished. "First thing in the morning, I'll bring some things over to help you out."

"Thank you. I do like being here, with you."

Maggie looked into Emma's dark brown eyes and drowned in chocolate. "I love you being here. I've not had such a pleasant time as I have these last few days."

"Then we'll have to make sure we spend more time together."

"I would like that."

"So, a second date it is?"

"Yes." Maggie grinned. "Very much so."

"And soon."

20

THE BODY FOUND

E mma was not convinced about moving into her new house. In fact, she thought she was being damned stupid when a warm castle was available. Except she needed to put some distance between Maggie and herself before she went too far.

Funnily enough, the look she got from Maggie suggested she felt the same. Emma hadn't expected that. After all, they hardly knew each other. Yet, when she thought of Maggie, her whole body felt light, and she a glow of happiness suffused her entire being. She'd never met anyone like Maggie. She liked everything about her. Maggie was attractive, had a great sense of humor, was undeniably intelligent, and had a warmth of personality that she liked a lot. All the things she liked in a person, in fact. And if that wasn't enough to scare her half to death, she was rich and a lord to boot.

Therein lay her problem. It would have been easier if Maggie had been an ordinary woman. The poor, normal woman next door would have been ideal. If anything, the title and the lands did not appeal at all.

But enough woolgathering. She was here now, and she had things to do.

The weather wasn't as cold as it had been, and a warm sun shone through breaks in the clouds and brightened the world outside. Inside, however, the house maintained an air of cold misery. It had been empty for so long that the whole fabric of the house seemed chilly and damp. A fire would have helped, but outside, the diminished woodpile contained logs so sodden they would be useless for weeks.

She remembered that one of the shops had displayed nets of logs and kindling. Maybe when she could, she'd go to the store and buy a few. That would be a good idea. Maybe later, after she'd unloaded everything from the car.

Emma had unloaded most of what she'd brought when the first police car went past. It arrived in the village with flashing lights and blaring sirens, racing by the house and under the gatehouse. She stared at the vehicle as it sped along the driveway to the hall. A few minutes later, a second vehicle flew by, followed soon after by an ambulance. Both of them sped toward the hall. The last car, a small van, pulled up outside the gatehouse and blocked the way.

"Maggie," Emma breathed. She stormed over to the gatehouse and didn't even care that she'd left her car and her front door open.

An officer stood in front of the van like a sentinel and intercepted her path. "Sorry ma'am," he said, his voice deep and hard. "You can't be going up to the hall right now."

"I don't care! Is Maggie...Is Lord Durrant all right?" she asked. "What's happened?"

"I'm sorry. I have no information at this time. Perhaps it would be better if you went home. I'm sure it will all be clear later."

Emma wasn't sure what to make of his comment, but she turned around, ready to walk back to Maud's house. She stopped abruptly when she found her neighbors all standing around the green, silently watching her, as though she'd done something wrong. She stared back for a moment, then walked back to her house, ignoring them all.

"That's a fine way to make friends and influence people," she said to herself, but she was too worried about Maggie to care. She plopped herself down on the sofa, and even though she'd vacuumed it twice, she still wasn't sure it was clean enough. She sat there until the chill of the house grew to be too much, then she went back outside. The police van remained at the gatehouse. She watched for a while, but other than the van and the police officer, there was little else to see, and she returned to the house to brew and stew about matters.

About mid-afternoon, a knock at the door dragged Emma from her reverie. Emma opened the front door, and the Maggie who stood on the doorstep was not the same woman she'd seen at breakfast. Dull eyes looked out from beneath the fringe of her hair, and the baggy sweatpants and tee shirt didn't do her justice.

"Oh, luvvie, are you all right?" she asked. "Come in. What happened? Are you hurt?"

"No, I'm fine," Maggie answered. "I'm not hurt in any way. I don't know. It's all such a mess. I can't believe this is happening."

Emma took Maggie's hand and led her into the kitchen. "Come sit down. I'll make you some tea. Have you eaten?"

"Eat? I can't eat right now."

"Tea, then."

"That would be lovely, thank you."

The tall, confident woman she knew had disappeared. Slumped in the chair, her elbows on her knees, Maggie sat as though her body were too heavy to lift. She stared at the floor, but Emma wasn't sure if she actually saw anything.

She made the tea and fretted as she added sugar to Maggie's' drink. Sweet tea was the only thing she could think of to help. She put the tea cup in front of Maggie and took a seat next to her.

"So, what's happened?" Emma urged. She took hold of Maggie's hand and squeezed. "Tell me all about it, honey."

Maggie sighed. "They found... I found a body."

Her first thought was that Maggie was trying to be funny. People only found bodies on televisions shows. "What?" she asked, as though that would give her time to think. A body? There had to be some mistake.

"Yes. In the cellar."

"How? Who?"

"I don't know. The police think I killed him."

"Don't be silly. There's no way they could think it was you."

"They do."

"How do you know? Have they arrested you? Cautioned you?"

"No. But the two detectives, Tallins and Peters, are convinced of it. I can see it in their eyes."

"They think nothing of the sort." Emma paused.

"There are strange things that happen at the hall, Emma. Things you haven't seen, and the whole situation looks odd."

"What strange things?"

Maggie didn't answer. She shook her head and looked miserable.

Emma didn't know what to think, but at the same time she couldn't let Maggie think she wasn't there for her. "It doesn't matter what they think. Right now, you are here with me and you're safe."

"I didn't want to impose on you, but there's nowhere else I can go."

"You're welcome here. You're always welcome. Do you want to talk about it?"

"It was so awful," Maggie whispered. Then she would say no more.

"Why were you in the cellar, Maggie?"

"The light had broken, so I thought I'd replace the bulb to make sure no one fell down the stairs. When I looked…when I looked, there was blood everywhere."

She shuddered as she spoke. "I didn't see it at first. I thought it was muck. The steps were broken, of course—I knew that—but I slipped… on blood. His blood. His face was a mess… blood everywhere…all over the floor... all over me."

"It's okay." Emma moved around the table and put her arms around Maggie.

"They took my clothes."

"I think it's procedure." She kissed the top of Maggie's head.

"Is it?"

"Yes," she said confidently. Although the only thing she really knew about police procedure was what she had watched on television dramas. "I saw an ambulance. I was worried that you were hurt."

"No, I'm fine. I'm not hurt."

"Why did they call the ambulance?"

"They said it's procedure," Maggie stated flatly. "As soon as I called emergency services and said there was a body, they had to send the police as well as an ambulance. Apparently they have to get a medical person to see if the victim can be saved. The preservation of life and so on is most important, they said."

"And?"

Maggie leaned deeper against Emma. "They pronounced him dead. It sounds so cold, so technical, when they say things in such a way."

"So what happens next?"

"I have no idea. The detectives say it's a suspicious death so they have to investigate. They need to identify him, run tests around the house and work out what happened."

"You poor soul," Emma soothed. "Is there anything I can do?"

It took a while before Maggie answered. "Can I stay here with you? The hall is full of all those crime people, so I can't be there right now. The police don't know what to do with me, so I said I would stay here with you. I have nowhere else to go. Is it all right?"

"Of course, it's all right."

"I don't need to be at the farm. Mr Jackson has everything under control. I could maybe help you out round the house."

"Of course, sweetheart, you stay right here."

"I mean, I should have asked you first, before I told the police, but you were the first person I could think of."

"You can stay with me as long as you want." She thought for a moment. Maggie needed distractions right now as the troubles of the day sank in. "I think you need things to do, so we'll go to the store, get a sack of logs and whatever else we need to get the fire going, and then you can show me what to do. How's that for starters?"

"Sounds good. I can do that."

"We can make this place all homey."

"All right. If you don't mind."

Emma lifted Maggie's chin so they could look each other in the eye. "Of course, I don't mind. I would love to have you here with me."

"Are you sure?"

"I'm sure."

21

SUSPECT

Maggie's nerves started to fray the sixth time the two detectives, Tallins and Peters, visited her that first day. They knocked on Emma's door as though prepared to knock it down. When Maggie answered, they strode into the house as though they were entitled. As soon as they appeared, Emma went into the kitchen and Maggie heard the click of the kettle being switched on.

"Just a few questions," Tallins said.

"You've already asked me lot of questions, and they aren't always different."

"Do you know the man in the cellar, Miss Durrant?" Peters asked her.

"No," she replied.

"About the image of the coffin drawn onto the door," Tallins pressed. "It's a bit funny that, since a man is dead there."

Maggie shrugged. "What can I say? Coincidence?"

"There are no such things as coincidences, Miss Durrant. We'd settle for the truth," Peters said. "The truth is always a good place to start."

"I've been telling you the truth," she answered. Although

how was she supposed to tell them the marks were the result of a stroppy ghost? They'd lock her up for sure.

"Where were you between the hours of two a.m. and seven a.m.?" Tallins asked.

"Bed," she replied.

"Can anyone verify that?" Tallins asked.

Maggie didn't dignify the question with an answer.

Peters took over. "We're now looking at a broader picture. Where were you between the hours of six p.m. and six a.m.?"

"At home."

"Can anyone verify this? Was Charles Durrant home?"

"No, he wasn't there."

"Where is your brother, Ms. Durrant?"

"No idea," she answered.

"So no one can verify where you were?"

"I was home, I said so before."

"So you did, but—"

"I was there as well," Emma said. She placed a tray with tea and biscuits on the coffee table. "You chaps visit so often I thought you'd like a cuppa."

"Why didn't you mention that before?" Peters asked.

"You never asked me," Emma answered. "Besides, I didn't think you were seriously treating Maggie as a suspect. Anyway, you know now. I was there all night."

The detectives looked at each other, and in that one look exchanged a whole world of meaning. One of them made a note in his little notebook, and they left.

Even so, the detectives weren't done with them. They knocked on the front door again a little after dark. Maggie yawned as she opened the door.

"Evening," she said. Emma stopped just behind her.

"Evening, detectives," Emma said.

"Miss Durrant, Miss Blewitt. We're done for today, but we'd prefer it if you didn't go to the hall just yet. We're still gathering evidence, and it would be best if you found an alternative venue to sleep." Detective Peters smirked. "I'm sure Miss Blewitt can accommodate. Either way, please don't go far. We may have more questions for you tomorrow."

"Good night, detectives," Emma said, and closed the door as they left.

"I'm sorry to put you through all this, Emma."

"It's not your fault. Look, stay with me as long as you need. Facilities are a little basic, but you're welcome to everything I have."

"I don't want to put you to any trouble."

"Trouble? How could I refuse you when you never once refused me anything? But perhaps I best not tell the police you threatened me with a shotgun."

Maggie looked horrified at first, and then she laughed. "Now that *would* put the cat amongst the pigeons, wouldn't it?"

"Think I should call them and let them know?"

"Yes. Go put me out of my misery. They want to lock me up, you know."

"Bully for them, then. Shall I open the wine?"

"You're not taking this seriously."

"Yes, I am, but there is nothing we can do about it right now. Might as well make the most of your freedom while you have it. We'll sit by the fire, relax, and have a glass of wine. We've done enough work around the house for today."

"Yes, well, I think I need a glass and then some."

Emma poured two glasses of red. "We'll be comfy enough, now we have a fire. And food."

"It makes a difference, for sure," Maggie said.

"We have to thank old Maud, who not only hoarded more tinned food, toilet roll, and bed linen than the armed forces, but also stocked us up on gin, brandy, and a bottle or two of sherry."

"She had wine as well?"

"Oh, no, I got that from the store earlier when we fetched the wood."

"Right." Maggie raised her glass. "Here's to your Aunt Maud."

"Absolutely."

22

ALONE IN THE BEDROOM

Emma realized, as she stood alone in the master bedroom, that this was going to be the first night in her new house. It was strange to think she'd come here at first with the intention of selling up. Now, she thought of this house as much her home as her apartment in the city. She liked the space here, for a start, and even though the house was small, it offered more than what her apartment had.

Then she shivered. Even though they'd had the fire going downstairs, the heat hadn't done much upstairs. She'd never been so cold.

"It's freezing in here," she said, needlessly because no one could hear. It would be worse in the winter, she thought, but even autumn in the mountains was colder than she had expected.

"What did you say?" Maggie called from her room.

Emma opened her bedroom door. "Cold," she shouted across the landing to Maggie. "I'm certain I shall freeze to death."

"No, you won't," Maggie bellowed back. "There's no ice yet."

"Yet," Emma mumbled to herself. She smiled as her

fingers brushed across the edge of the metal bedstead. Was this an antique, or just worn and old? She had no idea. The bedside lamp looked as though it should be condemned, and the fan didn't heat the room but turned cold air into a cold draught. The ceiling light hardly added any light, and when she reached out, shadows seemed to stretch out from her hands.

Nonetheless, the mattress on this bed was new. It still had the wrapping on it, and Emma decided to leave it that way.

"Still cold?" Maggie said from the door way.

"Yes, aren't you?"

"You'll harden up in a few days, and by this time next year, you'll not believe you ever thought it cold."

Emma laughed. "Yeah, right, and I'll be wearing thermal undies and thick jumpers."

"There you go. Country girl already."

Emma pulled back the curtains and stared out into the street. The warm glow of fires and lights from the surrounding houses were reassuring. Without clouds, it was brighter than it had been the last time she had looked out these windows. Stars littered the sky in a delicate pattern of bright and twinkling lights. The moon, although not full, was high and bright enough to cover the ground with radiant silver. Even with the moon, the gatehouse to Magwood Hall looked stark and black against the silver-tinted road. "It's beautiful out, but the moon makes everything look frosted."

At the center of the green, the old withered tree stood alone. With every gust of wind, the branches danced with dark menace and shook defiant, woody fists at the sky. And then, as she watched the branches sway, she blinked. For one moment, there was just the tree, and the next, a figure, all in white, stood still and unmoving against its dark trunk. The woman stared up at Maud's house, and Emma knew she was looking right at her. She knew it.

She stepped away from the window so fast, she bumped

into the dressing table. Her hairbrush and makeup bag rolled to the side and fell to the floor with an overly loud *thunk.* The mirror rocked, and she grabbed it just before it fell.

"Emma?" There was a short pause, then the sound of feet padding across the hall to her room. "Are you all right?" Maggie stood in the doorway but didn't step inside. The door frame stood like an invisible barrier that she couldn't cross.

Emma took a few breaths to steady herself. "Maggie, come look at this."

"What's the matter?" she asked as she entered the room. She bent down near the table and picked up the spilled makeup bag and brush.

"Not that. Look out here," Emma said. She'd turned away for only a second, but when she looked back to the tree, there was no one there.

She leaned against the window sill and rested her forehead against the cold glass. "I could have sworn there was someone, a woman, standing beneath the tree…" Her voice faltered. She could see Maggie's reflection in the window. She stood inches away and looked over Emma's shoulder.

Maggie's arm brushed against her, and Emma could no longer think of anything outside. Maggie's strength and body heat pulled her backward, like a magnet, and she could not resist the force of her presence. She leaned back until they were almost touching.

"Was it like the woman who flew across the window?" Maggie asked, her voice low, almost a whisper.

"Yes. I didn't make it up."

"No, I don't suppose you did."

"What do you mean?"

"Never mind," Maggie smiled, and her reflection smiled with her. "No one is there now."

"No, but it's not just this. Everywhere I go, it seems there is someone watching me."

"Paranoid, too."

"Pah! Magwood Durrant, you should go to your cold bed right now if you're not going to be helpful, or at least sympathetic."

Maggie didn't move. Instead, she wrapped her arms around Emma and hugged her. "I'm sorry. It's been a very difficult day."

Emma couldn't say a word at first. She wrapped her fingers around Maggie's arms so she couldn't get away. Her thoughts raced, but most of all she didn't want this contact to stop.

"Are you all right there?" Maggie asked.

"Maggie," Emma said as she leaned into her arms. She sighed. "Yes, I'm fine. I didn't mean to be so insensitive. It's all been very strange of late, and I'm not at my best. You've had a rotten day."

"Yes," Maggie agreed. "It could have been better."

"I'm right here for you, if you want to talk."

"Thank you, but I'd rather not think of anything at the moment. When I think about this morning…"

She shuddered so hard Emma felt her body shake. "It's all right, Maggie. It'll get better now."

"I hope so." Maggie took a deep breath. "Talking of strange. There's an interesting and upsetting story associated with that tree."

"Is there? Is that why no one has chopped it down," Emma asked. She stared out of the window, but didn't break contact with Maggie. "It looks diseased or something."

"It is, kind of. The tree is the village's dirty little secret." Maggie smiled, but there was little humor in it. "It's a scary story."

"Tell me. I like a good scary story."

"Long ago, it's said a local woman, no more than a girl, got herself pregnant, and not only did the father of the baby reject her, so did the whole town. They vilified her, called her many things, all of them unpleasant."

"Like what?"

"Devil's whore. Witch. That kind of thing."

"Nasty."

"Yes, they treated her so badly she killed herself, hanged herself from that tree, the very same one you see. Some say she didn't kill herself but was actually put there, on the tree, as a warning."

"A warning? About what?"

"I don't know."

"So she was murdered or something? On the tree there?"

"Uh huh."

"What happened to the baby? Did the baby live?"

"Legend says–"

A loud crack resounded from outside, and Emma jumped. When they looked through the window, the largest branch from the tree lay on the village green beneath it. Neither spoke at first.

Then Emma chuckled. "Bloody hell, Maggie. If you wanted to scare me, it worked."

"That's not the scary part."

"Then what is?"

"The legend is that the hanged lady appears in the days before the death of a Lord of Magwood Hall."

"No."

"Yes. So if you're seeing ghosts, then I'm not long for this world."

Emma snorted. "You're pulling my leg."

"Turn," Maggie instructed, and as one they about- faced to the fireplace. "The man who did the dirty was the man in the picture there."

"For real?" Emma's voice had risen a full octave. "And the woman?"

Maggie pointed at the other picture. "The late, great Emily Tapper."

"Seriously?"

"Now you know. I'm haunted by the ghost of your ancestor for something my ancestor did."

Emma couldn't help it, she laughed. "Magwood Durrant, you had me going there." She slapped Maggie's arm, but there was little force in it. "I don't believe in ghosts. And you've concocted quite a story."

"It's village legend. And it's true."

Emma shook her head and slipped her arm around Maggie's waist. "Well, never mind ghosts," she said after a while. "After a day like you've had, I bet you're exhausted."

"Yes," Maggie agreed, but she did not step away. Instead, she stepped closer, so she could hold Emma against her chest.

Emma rested her head against Maggie's shoulder and slid her other arm around Maggie's waist. They were so close she could smell the warmth of Maggie's skin mixed with soap.

"Emma, are you all right?"

"I am now."

Maggie chuckled. "We need to sleep."

"Yes, but you have to let me go first."

"Do I have to?" Maggie smiled, but her hands dropped to her sides.

Emma looked into Maggie's eyes, and she almost lost herself in the glinting blue made dark in the dimness of the room. She stood on tiptoes and kissed Maggie on the lips. "Goodnight, Maggie. You should go to bed and get some rest."

"You're making this very hard for me."

"Good."

"Goodnight, Emma. I'd best go."

Emma wanted to ask her to stay. She stared at Maggie for a moment. "This is not the best time, is it?"

"No, I suppose not."

"Goodnight, Maggie. Sleep well."

A short while later, Emma lay in bed, restless, and the chill of the sheets didn't help. The weight of all the blankets she'd added pinned her down, but even so, she couldn't sleep. She stared at the ceiling and listened to Maggie toss and turn in the room across the way.

She got up, padded across the landing to the other room, and in the dark, could see Maggie in bed. "Maggie?" she whispered. "Are you awake?"

"No, I'm asleep."

"Good," she said, and walked to the side of the bed. "Come to my room. We could keep each other warm, and we won't both fit in your bed."

Maggie sat up.

Emma held out her hand. "I'd rather like a cuddle. And I think you need one, too."

Maggie threw back the bedding and slid out of bed. "I thought you'd never ask."

"But no snoring. Otherwise, you can go right back to your own bed."

23

A DURRANT IN A TAPPER'S HOME

It was early, a little after dawn, and Maggie stood in the lounge area of Maud's house. She held a cup of tea in one hand and a slice of toast in the other. Upstairs, Emma was asleep, as usual. It was funny how it had taken a mere week to slip into a domestic routine, as though they'd been like this for years. With a Tapper, too.

She stared into the street as a car pulled up to the kerbside. Two men got out and approached the house. Maggie popped the last piece of toast into her mouth and opened the front door before they knocked.

"Morning," the men said, in unison.

"Good morning, Detective Tallins, Detective Peters. How very wonderful to see you," she said, without allowing them passage. "What can I do for you today? It has been hours since last we spoke."

"Can we come in?"

"Why?"

"Is Miss Blewitt here also?"

"She's asleep upstairs, like most normal people at this time of morning."

"I'm surprised you're still here. We opened the hall several days ago," Tallins said.

"I know." Maggie wasn't going to make it easy for them. "I wanted to make sure I didn't get in your way." What she didn't want to admit, even to herself, never mind the police, was that she was more than happy staying in this small house with Emma.

"Can we come in?" Detective Peters repeated.

"Yes, provided you don't disturb Emma. It's been a trying few days." She turned around and walked into the kitchen.

Once there, she selected one of the chairs and made herself comfortable. "Right, then. You're inside the house, I'm here, and you don't arrive at this hour unless you want to make sure I don't get away. That said, what are you going to accuse me of now?"

"Nothing. Is that a guilty conscience at work?" Peters asked.

Maggie sighed, and folded her arms across her chest.

"We're here as a courtesy, to bring you up to date," Tallins said.

"I see, no ulterior motive at all."

"We're just trying to do our job, Miss Durrant," Tallins added. "And we know you're out at the farm all day, so it's easier for us to find you before you go into the hills."

"Of course. How can I help?"

"The man in cellar?" Detective Tallins prompted.

"Yes."

"You said you didn't recognize him," he said.

Maggie didn't think it was a question, but she answered anyway. "No, I didn't, but as you might recall, detectives, his face was a little difficult to identify when I found him."

"Does the name Barry Swift or Weasel mean anything to you?" he pressed.

She thought of the name for a few seconds. "Nope," she answered. "Should it?"

"You tell me."

"No, detective, you tell me. I've already said I don't recognize the name."

"Do you like to gamble, Miss Durrant?" Peters asked.

She snorted. "If you looked at my finances you would know I don't have the cash for such frivolity."

"Yes, we have ascertained as much," Peters said, "But what about cash income?"

"Do you patronize, or have you ever, the Broadway Casino, about five miles or so north of Moorville?" Tallins asked.

"No."

"Do you know, or have you ever met, a man called Miles Orson, who runs this casino?"

"No."

Peters nodded. "Barry Swift has a history associated with the casino, namely debt collection and as a sometimes enforcer."

"I see. So you wonder if I am a gambler, because then I would have a reason for harming Barry Swift?"

Neither of them answered.

"Very well. I don't gamble, I never have, and I never will. It's a mug's game." She smiled. "I played snap once, as a kid. Does that count?"

Neither commented. They stood stony-faced and unmoving. She knew she was supposed to fill in the silence and incriminate herself.

"So this chap, Swift, is a thug for a casino. Obviously, he is known to you. Either way, he was in my home without permission and that, to me, suggests he was after whatever he could steal."

Peters frowned at her. "What about your brother?"

She laughed. "Best ask him, don't you think?"

"Maybe you and Swift came to an arrangement to cover your brother's debts?" Tallins asked.

"What a silly idea," she scoffed. She thought about his fine clothes and their often-hostile exchanges. "No, that would never happen."

"Where is your brother?" he pressed.

"I've no idea. He's an adult, and I'm not my brother's keeper."

Neither of the detective said anything, but they looked as though they were waiting for her to say something.

"So, where does this knowledge leave me?" Maggie asked.

"Can I be honest with you, Miss Durrant?"

"Please do, Detective Tallins."

Tallins glared at his colleague before he went on. "As you know, the steps into the cellar are not in the best condition.

"Tell me something I don't know."

"You should get them looked at."

Maggie shrugged. "They're on the to-do list."

"Looks like he slipped off the steps. Experts think it was about four steps down."

"So he fell," Maggie said.

"Or was pushed," Tallins added. "Either way, the pathologist reports that the cause of death was a blow to the head that fractured his skull. What confused the issue was that he had been strangled, too. The marks around his throat were clear."

"What?"

"In this case, it looked as though his death wasn't entirely accidental, so, you can understand our dilemma. After analysis at our labs, the current view is that the strap from his backpack caught on the newel post on the stairs. He slipped in the dark and panicked, started to strangle himself, and in the struggle to release the strap, fell down the steps to his death."

Maggie tried not to grin. "In other words, the official view is that I had nothing to do with it."

"Not as far as we can tell, not yet," Peters said.

"Given what we know, so far, we do no longer view the death of Barry Swift as a suspicious death. However, the circumstances are, and we will always look closely at any death that results from criminal activity."

"His? Or do you still think that I am committing some as-yet unknown crime?"

Tallins frowned and continued. "It is, we think, a series of unfortunate events, and we are looking no further. At least, not here in Castlecoombe. There are questions still to be answered, but that should have little bearing here."

"I see. Are you certain? I don't really want to have to answer so many questions every day at dawn, and I bet you don't want to drive here this early."

"You're not kidding," Peters grumbled, a little too loudly.

"Our final report will say that the evidence we collected suggests he was here to commit burglary, and in the act of concealing his presence, met with an unfortunate accident," Peters recited. "We have no evidence to the contrary."

"Good," she said.

"You can return to the hall," Tallins informed her, "but it's probably best to stay out of the cellar until it's cleaned and made safe."

"Well, when someone pays for the repairs, I'll get them done," she said.

Peters shrugged. "If there is anything more you need to ask, you have my card."

"I do." She showed them out of the house and was quite glad when she shut the door on them.

"Who was that?" Emma called from the top of the stairs.

"The police."

"What did they want this time?"

"Nothing. They wanted to tell me they no longer think I'm a murderer."

"Hey, Miss Innocent," Emma said as she came down stairs. She was still in her dressing gown.

Maggie quite liked seeing Emma in her dressing gown, but this time, she had pajamas on underneath.

"Have you made coffee yet?"

Maggie chuckled. "No. I made tea, though. I thought it was too early for you to be up, and I was about to leave for the farm."

"What did you have for breakfast?"

Maggie shrugged.

"You should eat something."

Maggie took two strides forward and kissed Emma's forehead. "You're adorable when you worry."

Emma huffed. "Am I not adorable at any other time?"

"Yes, of course you are. I'll get something to eat at the farm," she said.

"Are you sure?"

"Yes, I'm sure. Don't worry so."

"I do, though. I do."

Maggie tore her gaze away from Emma and looked at her watch. "I'd love to stay, but I have to get to work."

"I know."

"And I think I should move back to the house. I don't want to impose on your hospitality indefinitely."

Emma smiled at her. "You know I enjoy your company. You can stay here as long as you like."

"It'll be better if I go back."

"Oh, okay. Of course. You live at the hall, not some small house in the middle of a terrace."

"Your house in the middle of the terrace is very comfortable and appealing."

Emma nodded. "Now, don't forget, we're due another date night, aren't we?"

"We do, and we need to talk. There are things I need to discuss with you."

"That sounds ominous."

Maggie almost made it to the door. "Not to worry. Have you decided whether to stay here in Castlecoombe or not?"

"Not yet. To be honest, I haven't thought about it much. But I'm finding more reasons to stay."

"I don't want you to leave." Maggie looked at the floor, almost like a shy school girl. "Emma, have dinner with me Saturday night. At the hall."

"I would love to have dinner with you. Is this an actual date?"

Maggie grinned. "7:30 pm then, and you can stay at the house if you don't want to drive back afterward. I think you should stay, so we can have a glass of wine or two. I wouldn't like you to drive at all."

"Staying with you makes perfect sense. Now that the eyes of the law see you as innocent, we should celebrate."

SECRETAIRE

O f the veritable hodgepodge of furniture the Tappers had accumulated over the generations, few pieces were worth keeping. The *secretaire* bureau, tucked away in the corner, was a different matter altogether, and Emma had loved it on sight.

Tall and fashioned out of beautiful dark wood, it glowed with an inner luster that could not be faked. Inlaid with woods of almost every hue and trimmed with brass, the different-colored woods formed complex and intriguing shapes and designs. The top dropped down to reveal drawers and dividers, each one of them inset with a smaller and more intricate version of the external designs. Emma brushed her fingers over the warm softness of the wood and reveled in its smoothness.

She sat in a narrow chair and opened the bureau so she could look closer. Inside the drawers and partitions, Emma found copies, or originals, of all the papers she had in her own bag. In addition, she found a block of quality writing paper, a couple of cheap biros, a much older fountain pen shaped like a fattened missile, and a bottle of black ink. The writing surface, all worn green leather roughened with age, was still useable, but it needed to be replaced or restored.

"You're a beautiful desk," she said aloud, and smiled.

The fountain pen jerked upright, seeming to jump up and down, its hard lacquered shell clacking as it bounced on the wood.

"Good God!" Emma cried, and clutched at her chest. "What the hell?"

The pen bounced on its bottom twice, swung about like a conductor's baton marking time, and then cracked an upright section between the drawers and the dividers. It repeated its movements, twice, then lay down, still and unmoving.

Emma pushed back on the seat and stood up. She stared at the pen and tried not to think too hard about what must be the start of a mental breakdown of some sort. She needed a drink.

As she turned away, the sound of tapping resumed and grew more insistent. She walked to the center of the room and the tapping grew almost frantic.

She stopped and turned. "What the hell is going on?"

The torpedo jumped up and slid right across the writing surface.

"Stop."

More taps and slides ensued.

She reached out, but the energetic writing implement bounced once, then cartwheeled out of her way, rapped the wood twice, and settled down. Weird.

It crossed her mind, albeit briefly, that she should be scared. It had shocked her at first, but now it didn't seem at all odd. She was more than a little curious.

She waited for the pen to settle and slow and lashed out. Her fingers grasped empty air, and when she tried again, she got no closer than the first time.

"You shouldn't do that," she admonished.

The stylus leaned to one side and stood quivering.

"It's not right, you know. You should lie still like a normal pen."

The recalcitrant implement stood there, on end, but at least it was still. Emma fanned out her fingers and approached it with the care and attention reserved for a skittish animal. As she drew close, the pen trembled. She scared it.

Nonetheless, she managed to trap the pen in the corner of bureau. With deft and nimble fingers, Emma snatched up the wayward implement and shoved it in a drawer. "Gotcha." That she was talking to an inanimate object didn't warrant a second thought; it was already something she considered unexceptional.

She smirked with satisfaction. "I think I deserve a cup of tea."

In the kitchen, when she opened the door to get the milk, she allowed herself to be distracted by a bottle of wine. Tea, or wine? She grabbed the wine bottle and a corkscrew. Tea just wouldn't cut it for this. As she popped the cork, the sound of tapping in the drawer increased.

"All right," she yelled. "I'm coming."

The drumming stopped.

"After I've had my wine."

The drumming resumed, but with more insistence.

Emma sighed, took a good gulp of cool Viura, then left it on the kitchen table.

The drumming stopped as she sat down. "Okay. So what are you trying to tell me, Mr Pen?" She opened the drawer and released the implement onto the leather writing area. "I know I'm talking to an object, but hey, no one else is here so you will do."

Emma stared at the desk. "Were you trying to show me something?"

The pen stood to attention and leaned in her direction.

"I'll take that as a yes?"

A nod as it leaned forward again.

"The drawers?"

The pen fell over backwards.

"No?"

A nodded answer.

"There are easier ways than this," she said, and placed a piece of blank paper in the middle of the writing area.

The stylus fell over backward, and Emma was sure she heard a distant groan. "It's not the drawers and you can't write. Super," she muttered, and added a few curses. "There is something hidden here," she said as her fingers traced the inlay between the drawers. "I don't know what any of this means."

The pen bounced up and down, oozing excitement. "Here?" The pen bounced some more. "All right, then."

She traced the edges of the upright indicated. Nothing happened, but when she touched the rose-shaped inlay, the heart of the flower moved, or at least it appeared to move. She pressed harder and was rewarded with the sound of a muffled click. "There we go."

The sound of tapping drew her attention to the other upright, and now that she knew what she was looking for, Emma pressed the central part of the rose. Another slight click sounded, and at first, nothing changed. She ran her fingers across the wood, and the upright seemed a little proud of the drawers.

"Interesting," she muttered, and the pen nodded at her, as if it thought so, too.

Emma removed the four drawers and examined each one, noting as she did that the drawers were not as deep as she would have anticipated.

"*Very* interesting," she said, and looked into the holes made by the drawers. The insides were dark and she couldn't see much, so she grabbed the uprights and pulled. The drawer frame slid out.

At the rear, folded into the gap between the end of the drawers and the back of the bureau, Emma found a substantial sheaf of papers. As she brought them from their confinement into the light, a long sigh filled the room. "I guess this is what you wanted me to find, huh?"

Emma gathered the papers. There were quite a few sheets of cream-colored heavyweight paper, and all of them, except one, were covered in dense script. The almost blank one, no more than a title sheet, read "The Family Tapper, 1620."

25

SATURDAY NIGHT

Rather than use the kitchen entrance, Emma decided on a formal approach. She dropped her overnight bag on the step to the main door, rang the bell, and waited. Behind the door, she heard the bell reverberate with a deep, booming *ding dong*. It sounded nothing like the high-pitched tinkle or the buzzer effects she associated with a normal-sized house or apartment. Then again, this was a grand hall, a castle, and not some fifth-floor apartment. All she had to do now was wait. She was glad it wasn't raining as she stood before the entry, because Magwood was a large place and she had no idea how long it would take Maggie to answer.

Someone unlocked the door and opened it quicker than she'd anticipated, and she couldn't help but smile in anticipation.

The man who opened the door a moment later looked identical to Maggie, but wasn't her. Her grin wavered. "Hello," she said.

She'd not expected the resemblance between the siblings to be so great, and yet so very different. Both blond, yet his hair was bright and striking, hers was a shade softer. His eyes, bright and blue as the heart of a glacier, were nothing like the sun-drenched blue of Maggie's eyes. Her smile could melt ice, and his would make it form all over again. Maggie was the girl next door, so long as the girl next door was rich, lived in some huge hall, and owned everything in sight. He was nothing like her, and his cold gaze slid like grease over her skin.

"Yes?" he drawled.

The grin on her face vanished.

She pulled back her shoulders and spoke with as much confidence and assurance as she could manage. "You must be Charles. I'm Emma, and Maggie is expecting me."

"Well, well." He looked her up and down, and not only undressed her, but suggested something sordid as well. "You're the Tapper. The one who's got Mags' knickers in such a twizzle."

Emma bristled. She couldn't help it. He made everything sound dirty, and there was nothing dirty or nasty about Maggie, nor their relationship. "Yes, I suppose I am."

He lifted one eyebrow as though surprised by her reply.

Even such a small gesture annoyed her. "I suppose I am the Tapper, and last of my line. But I've not seen Maggie's knickers, so I have no idea whether they are in a twizzle or not. But," she smirked, "it does sound a pleasant challenge. Maybe I'll find out later, after a bottle of wine or two." She was surprised she didn't blush, but she was so angry she didn't care what anyone thought.

His leer broadened. "So you do plan to sleep with her, then," he whispered as she passed.

Emma thought about saying something witty and sharp, but all she could manage was a bitter, "You're too late to worry about such things."

Maggie strode across the hall in a fitted trouser suit. Her damp hair clung to the side of her face and she looked angry enough for two.

"Hi, Emma," Maggie said. Her usually smooth voice

sounded cold and strained with barely suppressed anger. She glared at her brother. "Charles, you were raised with better manners than this."

"Hello, Maggie," Emma said, interposing herself between the two Durrants. "It's all right."

"So, now you've met my brother," Maggie said. She ignored him.

Emma nodded.

"Charles, are you going out this evening?"

"What's it to do with you?" he snapped.

"I just want to know," Maggie said.

"It's none of your business. However," he said, with a leer, "I'm not sure I'll bother going anywhere. I think I'll stay with you two."

"No, go," Maggie commanded.

He smirked.

"Maggie, it's fine," Emma said. "We'll need a waiter to serve the food and clear up after us, won't we? I don't mind if Charles fills in as one. I'm sure he'll manage. What do you think?"

"I'm no waiter," he sputtered.

Maggie kept her face blank. "But Charles, Emma is right, your presence as a waiter would make things so much easier. What a great idea."

"I'm going out," he growled. "Back when I feel like it." He stormed through the house, and the two women looked at each other. Maggie snickered.

"Maggie, I know he's your brother, but I am glad he's gone. I don't think he likes me."

"It's not you. He's going through something I don't understand, and he's in a bad mood. It can take a while to get used to him."

Emma was not so sure.

"I heard what he said."

"You did?"

"Yes." Maggie smiled. "I heard what you said, too."

"I see." Now the blush finally made its appearance.

"Never mind him, or what was said." Maggie smiled sweetly. "Are you hungry?"

"Yes."

"Good, come on through to the kitchen. I did think about setting up the formal dining hall, but resisted the temptation to show off. Besides, I'd be happier eating in the kitchen. The table and chairs are very comfortable there. Is that all right with you?"

"Of course. I like the kitchen. It's more informal, and I think I'd be a little off put by some fancy hall."

"Good, then it's settled."

"Besides," Emma said, "isn't the kitchen where the wine is kept?"

Maggie laughed and led the way into the kitchen. "I like a woman who has the right priorities in life." She held the door open for Emma to go through first.

"Take a seat, and make yourself comfortable. It's all ready," Maggie said.

The aroma of cooking food and heat from the range filled the room. "It smells divine."

Maggie filled two bowls with soup and served them with thick wedges of homemade bread. "I hope you don't mind simple home-cooked food?"

"Of course, I don't mind."

Maggie poured two glasses of wine, and they sat together at the table. "I'm glad you could make it."

"I wouldn't miss this for the world," Emma said. She tucked into her soup and conversation drifted away.

"You're quiet, Emma."

"Hungry," she said, and finished her glass of wine. Maggie topped her glass up.

"You seem a little distant though. Thoughtful, even,"

Maggie said. "Are you upset or concerned about meeting Charles?"

Emma looked up and stared into Maggie's eyes. "No, it's not that. I admit, I'm a little preoccupied and uncertain about things."

"Oh? Is there something wrong?" Maggie asked. She cleared away the empty bowls and started to serve the main course. She put the pie in the middle of the table and when she cut through the golden pastry, all kinds of meaty aromas filled the air.

"Maybe. I don't know," Emma admitted.

"If something was wrong, you'd tell me, wouldn't you? Unless Charles upset you more than you let on and you don't want to say anything?"

"No, it's not Charles. He's the furthest person from my mind right now."

Maggie served her a large helping of the game pie and added vegetables. "You should try the pie."

Emma picked up her knife and fork and tried a little piece, but she barely tasted it. Her thoughts churned too much. She put her knife and fork down on the sides of her plate.

"Please, Emma, tell me what's wrong."

"You know me so well already, and it's one of the things that keeps my mind busy."

"How so?"

"I feel as though I have known you for years."

"Yes," Maggie said, simply. She sipped at her wine and looked at Emma. "I feel that, too. Is it a problem?"

"I don't know. Should it be?"

"Answering a question with a question isn't helping. Do you want to talk about it?"

Emma took a long sip of her wine and topped up her glass. "After dinner," she answered. "I think we should talk."

"Very well. Now I'm intrigued."

They exchanged a few more polite words, and then busied

themselves with eating dinner. Emma noticed Maggie wasn't eating much. "Are you not hungry, Maggie? You're picking at the food as though you're looking for something unpleasant in every bite."

"I'm not as hungry as I thought I was."

"Something on *your* mind?"

Maggie didn't answer the question. "We should go to the main hall. There's a nice fire going there, and we can chat if you like."

Emma wiped her mouth and placed her cutlery across the plate. "I'm done. Shall we wash up?"

"No, let's go into the other room."

When they made themselves comfortable in front of the fire, Emma helped herself to another glass of wine. She'd already drunk most of the bottle, but that didn't mean she needed to slow down.

"I know it's not my business, but you're drinking with rather more determination than usual."

"I don't care," Emma answered.

"All right." Maggie pulled her chair closer to her. "You didn't want to talk about anything earlier, but do you want to talk now?"

"About what?"

"About whatever it is that's bothering you."

Emma stared away for a moment, but looked back when Maggie reached across the distance between them and covered Emma's hand with hers. Emma looked at the long fingers, turned her hand over so they were palm to palm, and sighed.

"There is so much going on at the moment. I know you've had your share of trouble recently, too."

"I don't think this year has been easy for you, either," Maggie said.

She turned to look at the fire; she couldn't look at Maggie

whilst her thoughts turned in circles. Most of them barely made sense. "Perhaps not. It's all so confusing."

"What is?"

"First of all, I like you, Maggie and when we're together, I feel like we're more than just friends."

Emma paused to see if Maggie would comment, but she didn't, and Emma couldn't bring herself to look up to check her expression.

"I'm not sure what it means, or what it should mean," Emma continued, "but I've never shared my bed with a woman for a week in such a chaste fashion. We've not even had a proper kiss. I'm not sure if that's because I see more in this than you do. If I'm pushing myself on you when I shouldn't, then just say. You don't need to be that polite. Maybe you're just not interes—"

"That's not it," Maggie interrupted.

Emma looked up from the fire and stared into the depths of Maggie's eyes. "What is it, then?"

"It's complicated."

"That's a cop-out," Emma said.

"Not really, it's more a case of delaying tactics. There is a lot to consider, and I take these things slowly."

"Right. What does that mean?"

"It means if we get to share a bed, I want it to be for more than a cuddle."

Emma took a good long drink of her wine. "What's so complicated about that?"

"Well for one thing, you haven't said that you'll stay."

"Ahh, I see. You don't want to get involved with someone who doesn't want to stick around?"

"There is that," Maggie said.

"I can understand that. What else?"

"Did I say that there was another reason?"

"Not explicitly, but if you say 'for one thing,' then there must be another thing as well."

"I have to be sure, that's all." Maggie picked up her glass and sipped her wine. "What about you? From the depth of that frown on your face, I think there is something else on your mind. You said as much before we ate."

Emma laughed. She couldn't help it. "There are lots of things on my mind right now. One of them will make you think that I'm quite mad."

"No, I won't think that."

"I think my house is haunted," Emma said.

Maggie coughed and almost choked on her drink.

"See? I knew you'd think me silly."

"No, I don't. Not at all, but I think the jump from sleeping together to haunting caught me by surprise."

Emma stared into the depths of her glass, but she saw nothing except the remains of her wine.

"Tell me why you think there's a ghost."

"I didn't say anything about a ghost."

"Hauntings always involve ghosts," Maggie answered with a smug grin on her face. "Because I understand about such things. After all, I live in an ancient house, and there are ghosts everywhere."

"Do you?"

"Tell me what you saw," Maggie prompted. She looked at Emma with such focus. "Tell me about the ghost."

"If I hadn't seen it with my own eyes, I'm not sure I would've believed it. It was odd. And before you ask, it had nothing to do with drinking wine, either."

"I wasn't going to suggest it was."

"Good."

"Like I said, I know about ghostly things. I'll prove it." She stood up, walked to the window, leaned against a stone mullion, and waited. When Emma stood at the window next to her, Maggie pointed to the dark hills. "The Durrant estates are not extensive, but they are bound, to the north, by two large peaks known for nothing except the small vein of blue fluorspar running deep underground. Many lifetimes ago, they mined the mountain for the bluestone until not a bit was left in the veins they'd found."

"And they gave up?"

"Never." Maggie shook her head. "If there was one vein, there would be another. They just had to find it. They mined deeper and deeper, until one fateful night, the mine collapsed and trapped three miners in the depths. They say the ghosts of those miners can still be seen, toiling in and out of the mine, their lanterns rocking from side to side in the night. So if anyone is going to believe in ghosts, it will be someone like me."

"Have you seen the ghosts yourself?"

Maggie bit her lip. "Of the mine? No."

"So you don't believe me or believe in ghosts."

"I didn't say that at all. Of course I believe you." But Maggie looked distant and out of reach. "Ghosts are such a complex subject, you know. You should come to the library, and I'll show you. I have a pretty impressive collection of books dealing with ghosts, and the paranormal in general."

"Really?"

"It's been an interest of many of my forebears as well." She finished her wine and refilled both glasses.

"Have you actually seen any ghosts yourself?"

Maggie frowned. "I've encountered some events yes, but tell me about yours first, and then I'll tell you about mine."

"All right," Emma drummed her fingers on her thigh as she gathered her thoughts. Maggie seemed so diffident and controlled, perhaps she was too shy to expose herself to ridicule. Emma nodded; more to herself than anything else, she didn't mind if she went first. "It was the pen's fault. It wanted me to look at a special place inside the bureau, and it was most insistent I do so."

"The pen spoke?" The incredulity in Maggie's voice unmissable.

"Of course not. Pens don't actually speak—they don't have mouths for a start. They speak with the ink, though, in words, although this one wouldn't or couldn't write anything. It would have been so much easier if it had. Instead, it kept moving from side to side, and it upset me so much I locked it in the drawer."

"Next you'll say you smacked its arse and sent it to bed without any supper."

"Don't be facetious, Magwood Durrant. It's a fountain pen, not a child."

Maggie snickered and shook her head. "So, what happened next?"

"Well, it kept banging away, until the sound drove me mad and I let it out. Once it had my attention, it stood on end, waiting for me. Every time I spoke, it responded and moved until I understood what it wanted, and when I did, the house agreed."

"So you have a haunted pen and the house is sentient? Do I understand correctly?"

"I think so." Emma picked up her glass and swallowed half of the contents straight away. "You're not upset or freaked out by this at all. In fact, it's almost as though you expected it or something." Her eyes narrowed. "You know something. I know you do."

"What do you mean?" Maggie asked, and stared into her glass. No matter how hard Emma tried to look into her eyes, she avoided her gaze.

"Is this the ghost you've seen?"

Maggie shook her head. "I would have liked to have seen that, though. It sounds fun."

"Fun! I thought I was going mad."

"If we are talking about ghosts, there are other weird things, too."

"Yes?" Emma prompted.

"We've known each other for such a short while, and yet..." Maggie's voice faded away.

"But we are not strangers are we, Maggie? Not really," she said. She reached out and squeezed Maggie's cool fingers.

"No, we're not, I suppose. Have you ever dreamed of me, Emma?"

"What?"

"Did you dream of me before you came here?"

Emma stared through the window and into the darkness outside. Had she dreamed of Maggie?

"No," she answered, but in her heart, she wasn't sure if she was being entirely truthful. When she turned around, she saw disappointment on Maggie's face. "But when you hold my hand, I feel as though you've always held my hand. And then I never want you to let go. But I'm not sure you want the same thing. Do you?"

"It's not that simple." Maggie replied, but she looked distraught.

"You said you were reticent about us, or because there is something more?"

"Yes there is more, but I'm not sure I know how to explain."

"Try." Emma took a deep breath and stopped dead. "Is it me, or is it really cold in here?"

"It's not you," Maggie said, and wisps of steam came out of her mouth as she spoke. "Perhaps we should return to the fireside." She looked worried, though, and muttered quietly more to herself, "Not now," she said.

Emma wasn't really sure if she'd heard correctly, so she ignored it and strode across the room. The heat from the fire, the only source of heat in the room, took away the chill. She took a good gulp of wine and sat down. "Or maybe there is something else going on? Maybe it's all about the feud you have with the Tappers. Is this why you don't want to get involved with me?"

"It's—"

Emma interrupted her, "I thought this thing, this feud between the Tappers and Durrants, was all a bit of nonsense. But it isn't, is it?

"No, it's not, but you never mentioned anything about it so I didn't really know what you knew, or even if you were that interested."

"Of course I'm interested."

"More to the point, I've been putting it all off and delaying talking about it."

"That feud business shouldn't make a difference between us. Look, I didn't come here to fall for you, Maggie. I came to see my house, to see where I came from, and then sell up."

Maggie joined her and sat in the chair next to her. "Fall for me?"

"What? Yes, I thought that was obvious."

Maggie reached out and held Emma's hand. "*Feud* makes it all sound melodramatic and simple. It isn't. It's mad."

"I'm beginning to think that everything to do with Castlecoombe is nonsense, crazy, or downright insane. Anyway, this feud. When I heard about it all I wanted was to come here and see what it was all about, and then I could go back to where I belonged—the city. I wanted to see what the hell Maud meant when she passed the papers to me through the solicitors because it was like the ravings from a television show or something."

"What did she say?"

"Does it matter?" Emma shrugged.

"Yes. And no. I don't mean to push you away, I'm just cautious."

"Because I'm a Tapper, so you're not allowed to get close?"

Maggie toyed with Emma's fingers; her gaze focused on their hands so intently that Emma couldn't see her eyes.

"None of it made sense. It was, as I said, all a ranting and raving nonsense. A bitterness that stretched over generations. They reveled in every Durrant death, and I couldn't understand such animosity. At one point I thought it looked like a genetic problem, a Tapper madness, and I had yet to show the symptoms."

"Maud wasn't insane."

"Perhaps not, but I thought she was." She opened her handbag and pulled out the documents she had discovered to wave them at Maggie. "You've never told me about the extent of the animosity between your family and mine. Is that why you back away? Because I'm a Tapper? And don't say it's complicated."

Maggie looked at the documents. "It's compli–"

"Don't you dare," Emma interrupted. "This is a full account of my family's history, and it fills in the blanks Maud's book missed. I'm sure you can guess how it all starts."

"Yes, you're right. It all starts with Emily Tapper." Maggie looked thoughtful. "I'd like to read those, if I may."

"Maggie!"

"I'm not trying to delay, as such, but I would like to read them anyway, I'm just stating my interest."

"Fine. But now you need to tell me what you know. I can't see you being ignorant about such things."

Maggie's cheeks flushed. "The animosity between the Tappers and Durrants is well known, but the rest is hearsay. A myth passed down from one Durrant to another."

"And Maud?"

"Maud kept herself to herself and wouldn't speak to me or any of my relatives." Maggie looked away, her focus so distant Emma thought she was ignoring her. "Maud hated us with a passion. She and her sister drove my father mad. We have always known there was a problem between the families, but it had been brushed under the carpet, so to speak."

"You mean hushed up?"

"Yes, and it has taken several generations for us to try and piece it back together. It would have been easier if we could have talked to the Tapper family, but they would never have anything to do with us."

The fire grew more agitated and spat a coal at Maggie. "Shhh. Steady," she whispered, and with a pair of blackened tongs, put the coal back into the fire. She smoothed her clothing without thinking and wiped the black ash from her trousers.

"I'm sorry, Maggie, I'm having a tough time with all of this. There are so many things to know, and I feel lost and helpless because I know so little. The world, my world, is out of control, and I don't know what to do."

Maggie stood up, and for a moment, Emma thought she might be swept into a hug. Instead, she stood there, clenching and unclenching her fists.

"And then there is you." She gestured between them, "I'm so not sure what any of this means."

Maggie nodded. "All right."

Another coal spat out of the fire and landed at Maggie's feet. She didn't say a word, but scooped the coal from the rug with a small set of fireside tongs, and threw it back into the grate. She knelt beside fire and brushed the hot coals on the hearthstone towards the hearth.

"Today is not—" Maggie began. More coals jumped out of the fire, and no matter where she stood or knelt, they aimed straight for her. She cursed as she batted at the coals closest to her and tried to put them back into the fire.

"Are you hurt?" Emma asked.

"No, I'm fine."

"Today is not your lucky day, is it?"

"You're right. It isn't. There is no luck for a Durrant lord today." Maggie sighed. "This is one of those other complications. Today is my birthday—"

"You didn't tell me."

Maggie shrugged. "I'm selfish, and I wanted to spend time with you."

"That's not selfish? Maggie, why didn't you say?"

"Today, I'm thirty years old," she persisted, "and at some point between today and my next birthday, I will die."

"What? No, that's insane."

Maggie continued without looking at Emma. "Every Durrant firstborn has died at this same age. If not before. It is an inviolate fact of our lives, and no matter what, this will be my last year. I cannot change it. No one has ever changed it. And it's why I can't let you get too close. It would be selfish to hurt you when I know I won't be around for long."

"Maggie!"

"I've never been afraid of dying. It is what it is, and it's as much a part of my life as the hall itself. Maggie glanced at Emma and quickly looked away. "Until you came along. Now I have a reason to live, but it all seems futile. I cannot change what will be, and the reason is simple. At least, we Durrants think it's simple." She shrugged. "We are still paying the price for doing wrong by Emily Tapper."

"'A woman scorned is a curse that lives forever.' It was written on one of the sheets of paper I found today," Emma said.

"Exactly. You are my death."

Emma looked stricken for a moment, and then she burst out laughing. "Bloody hell, Maggie. You sound like Maud herself, and all the Tappers before her. There are no such things as curses. Curses are a gypsy thing to scare the gullible. Such things do not happen in the real world."

"Are you so sure, Emma?"

"Of course. You're pulling my leg. You had me going for a minute."

"What about haunted houses and pens that sit up and bow?"

"That's different. But curses are so dramatic. Like witches and demons, vampires and werewolves, they don't exist."

"You mustn't forget the gothic castle perched on the side of a mountain. You know, like this one."

"Now you're pulling my leg even harder."

"I suppose this is more neo-gothic," Maggie continued. "It's not old enough to qualify for gothic."

"Looks close enough to me. And there's no lightning or fog. Nothing odd."

"Except the night you arrived."

"Stop it. Now you're scaring me. I'll start looking for bats flying outside."

"I'm serious," Maggie said.

They were quiet, then, and sipped their wine.

"So, this curse is for real?" Emma asked.

"Yes." Maggie looked tired, as though she carried the weight of the world on her shoulders and she had given up trying to carry it.

"I still think it's nonsense. It has to be."

Maggie, once proud and tall, now sat hunched over and appeared diminished somehow. When she looked at Emma, her eyes were sad. "Do I look like I'm laughing?"

Emma looked, really looked, and the energy and liveliness she associated with Maggie had vanished. This was not the Maggie she knew.

"Today, I am thirty," Maggie continued, her voice tired and her shoulders slumped. "I am the eldest, the firstborn Durrant of my generation. You're the last of yours. Coincidence?"

Emma shook her head. "It's a scary coincidence, that's all and you're being morbid."

"Am I?"

"Yes, Maggie. What's truly scary is the fact we look like we are the first ones reincarnated. Now, that's spooky."

"You've proved my point, exactly."

26

I'LL SHOW YOU

Emma rose to her feet, took a deep breath, and wrapped her arms around Maggie's waist. She held on, even when Maggie stood so stiffly she could have been made of wood. She did not return the hug.

"I'm not sure this is wise," Maggie said. Her voice sounded cold, and as distant as the peaks.

"What's not wise? Why?"

"You know already."

"I don't know anything. But you seem to know everything, even when you say you don't."

"I can't...we can't."

"Why not? Because you've convinced yourself you're going to die?"

"You make it sound as though it is all in my head." Maggie grabbed her hand and stopped her from talking. "Come upstairs with me. I'll show you."

Emma stopped. "Er, show me what, exactly?"

"Everything."

Maggie looked quite determined.

"All right, then. Lead the way."

Maggie strode out of the room and didn't stop until she

reached the entrance hall. She paused with her foot on the first step, looked over her shoulder to see if Emma followed, and raced up the stairs.

"Where are we going?" Emma had to hurry to keep up.

"To the east turret," Maggie said. They moved swiftly up to the first floor, along the corridor, passed the room where Emma had stayed, to the door at the end. It looked like any other door along this corridor, but it didn't lead to a room. It led, instead, to a stone staircase. "It's blocked on the bottom floor," Maggie said. "I don't know why. That's why we access it from the end of the first floor and not the ground."

Unlike the main stairwell, with its decorative stonework and wood polished until it turned to a glassy sheen, these steps were plain and functional. There was nothing decorative to soften the stark stone. Their steps echoed through the stairwell as Maggie marched onward and now upward. Even the walls were plain, lime-washed and without pigmentation. The off-white walls looked dirty and unloved.

"Maggie, slow down. What's the rush? I can't keep up with you."

Maggie looked at her with distant eyes. "I'm sorry," she said, but even her words were lifeless and flat. She didn't react at all when the distant cry of a baby filled the space around them.

"Maggie?" Emma said as the cry intensified, and her steps shuddered to a halt.

"Ignore it."

"Maggie, it's a baby. Whose baby is it?"

"It isn't. It's not a baby," Maggie answered, and a cool wind wrapped around the inside of the stairwell. "We need to go now. Keep moving."

Emma shivered, but she wasn't sure if it was the drop in temperature or Maggie's impersonal and perfunctory demeanor. "It's cold here."

"It's always like that," Maggie explained. "Always."

"I don't understand."

"You will," Maggie muttered, and she continued up.

At the stop of the stairs, a solid, ironbound door with huge, dark hinges, blocked the way. A lock, all black, metallic, and rimy, shone in the starkness of the overhead lights.

Maggie rummaged in her pocket, drew out an oversized key, and wrapped the handle in a thick wad of linen.

"What a spectacular key."

"It's genuine seventeenth century. I mean all of it—the door, the key, and the lock. All of it."

"No one is getting through here without an invite."

"Exactly."

Emma reached out, and the chill of iced wood took the heat from her fingers. "What the hell? It's frozen!"

"Yes."

"I know it's not the height of summer, but how on this good earth can a door be frozen?"

"It's been like this for years, so far as I know."

"Years?" Emma pressed.

"Generations," Maggie answered. "Sometimes it gets worse."

"How can it get worse, and why?"

"Because it does, Emma. It just does."

"That's not an answer," Emma pushed, but that didn't stop the temperature from dropping even further. The walls were so cold, they sucked the heat from the stairwell in steamy trails. Goosebumps erupted over Emma's arms, and she shivered. "Are you going to open the door?"

"In a moment," Maggie answered. "This is why I cannot get close. I'll bring nothing good to anyone I meet, and I can't inflict pain like that on someone I care about."

Emma put her hand on Maggie's arm. "You don't, and you're starting to sound maudlin."

Maggie tried to smile. "You almost made me forget, but that would have been wrong."

Emma had just opened her mouth to speak when three huge drops of water, cold and dirty, fell on her face. "What the hell?"

Maggie glanced at the drops on Emma's face and nodded, as if she'd been expecting it. She put the key in the lock and worked it back and forth.

"Maggie? You're scaring me."

She stopped. "Let me put it like this—you have a haunted pen in a haunted house, but I'm the haunted heir to a failing and haunted estate. Does that help?"

"Not at all, Maggie. It doesn't matter to me at all."

"It does to me. I'm not going to be the one to break another Tapper heart."

With a little more effort, the key turned, and with a loud grinding *kerchunk*, the door swung open. Warm air rushed out.

"Come in, before it gets any worse," Maggie said, striding into the chamber.

Inside, Emma immediately forgot the chill and Maggie's off-hand manner. All of the east wing turret had been converted into a large, circular room, with so many lights it glowed. Above, the ceiling was several floors up, and rings of stone corbels marked where the other floors should have been. Vaulting, embedded in the walls, marked where doors might have opened onto other floors. Windows, all small and narrow, circled around the tower where these tower rooms would have been.

"It used to have several floors above, but they collapsed a long time ago and have never been repaired," Maggie explained. "I thought of having wooden stairs circling around the whole tower again, but I kind of like the open feel of this."

There was so much to see. The walls on the lower area were almost entirely covered in shelves filled with books. Above the books were dozens of pictures, all portraits.

A large table, covered in more books and note paper, stood

in the middle of the room. A fireplace with a step ladder stood off to one side, and other than a small writing desk and a couple of chairs, there was little else in the room.

Emma didn't know where to start. "That's a lot of books," she said.

"These are the family's collected works, but there are more in the library."

"Lots of portraits here, too."

"Yes, my family members. There are others around the house, as I'm sure you've seen."

"I have, but this is a very interesting collection."

"Yes," Maggie mumbled. She pulled a set of stepladders to one side of the wall and climbed to the top. "Never mind them. Look at this." She tugged at a sheet of cloth and with a soft swish, the fabric fell to the stone floor. Underneath, a square board, about twelve foot by twelve foot and decorated with a stylized tree, marked the full lineage of the Durrant family. "You have your lineage in your hands. This is mine."

"Look at the work that has gone into it," Emma breathed as she scanned the whole diagram. Names, relationships, and tiny images drawn to illustrate the names. "It's beautiful. Impressive."

"No, no, no," Maggie moaned. "Use the stepladders and look here, at the top. I need you to see all the important bits."

Emma climbed the steps. "Charles Magwood," she read aloud. She knew this part already. She'd read about it, about him, a few hours before.

"Just look."

Emma froze when she saw the cloud drawn around the names of Charles Magwood, Junior, and his wife. A name had been added with assorted images, including a demon with horns and a forked tail. She frowned. "I see you've added Emily to your tree."

"Yes," Maggie sounded relieved, now that she had exposed the portrait. "Can you see it?"

"I see that your ancestors have demonized her, painted her in as the bogeyman. With horns and a forked tail? How mature."

"Yes, but it was a different time, then, and witches and demons were a very real thing for them," Maggie said, relieved Emma understood. "Can you see the symbols that make her a witch? They have included the raised left hand, a goat's head, toadstools at her feet, a pentagram on her breast, and a crow on her shoulder."

Emma nodded. "Anything to diminish the fallen woman. Blaming her for what they did together. Sex out of wedlock was a big sin, even though many did it. And usually it was the woman who was blamed."

"Exactly."

"So they linked it to Charles Junior and his wife?"

"Yes, and along came a child," Maggie said.

"Oh."

"Now do you see the uncertainty of my heritage?" Maggie asked.

Emma made her way to solid ground before she answered, "No, I don't."

Maggie took a deep breath. "Your own great grandmother, Emily Tapper, may have also mothered the Durrant line. Why else mention Emily in the family tree? I know there was a child, a bastard born, and he, Charles, would have brought this child into the family. It seems to me that Emily is killing her own progeny for the hate of one man," Maggie whispered. "Now, here you are, another branch of her Tapper tree. The differences between these two branches are so slight, the animosity between our families should cease to exist. But it doesn't."

"What? You think we're related, so we can't be close?"

"Yes," Maggie hissed. "You are descended from Emily Tapper, and so…" She waved her hand about.

"Even if that were true, we are separated by many

generations. Good grief, Maggie, at the worst, it would make us very distant cousins, and no one would bat an eyelid at that."

Maggie nodded. "But now at least you know."

Emma's gaze skimmed lower, and a golden scroll marked where Edward Charles Magwood became Edward Charles Durrant. "I see the name change, but why, Maggie?"

"When they realized the firstborn Magwood sons and daughters all died rather young, they decided a new name might be more fortuitous."

"And was it?"

Maggie snorted. "Check the dates of birth and death of all the heirs. None of them live beyond thirty."

"I know."

"Is this all written in your records, too?"

"Yes, in part, and I went to the cemetery."

Maggie shrugged. "This is the curse of the firstborn. Emily Tapper has her revenge on all of her children."

"Nonsense. Besides, you're not descended from Emily Tapper."

"What?" Maggie answered. Her shoulders slumped for a moment, and then she jerked up and her eyes sparkled. "I'm not an Emily Tapper descendent?"

"No, Maggie, you're not. And neither am I."

27

TOWER

Emma glanced at several pictures on the walls around the tower room as she considered what to say next. "Have you ever wondered why all of you Magwoods or Durrants have blue or grey eyes?"

"What a strange but interesting question," Maggie said, as her eyes skimmed over the portraits in the tower. "What has that got to do with anything? And what has it got to do with the family tree?"

"And have you wondered why my family always has brown eyes?" Emma persisted.

"Tapper eyes are famous for being brown."

"It's almost as though our families didn't want to run the risk of ever being confused as being a member of the other family, isn't it?"

"Now you sound almost paranoid, Emma. There's no conspiracy." Maggie's words sounded firm, yet her voice betrayed her; she was not convinced.

Emma unrolled her papers. "Look, there's a note here. 'Brown are the eyes of the Tapper True.'"

Maggie snorted. "Aren't prophetic statements supposed to rhyme or something?"

"You're not taking this seriously, are you?"

"How could I not be serious about all this? It's my life destined to end early, so I think I have the right to indulge in a little frivolity."

"I'm sorry, Maggie. Really, I am."

"So what else does your sheaf of papers have to say about my family?"

"'Evil lies in eyes of blue, beware the Magwood.'"

"What!" Maggie looked shocked.

Emma laughed. "See, Tappers can be frivolous, too."

"That was dreadful."

"Yes, but you asked for it."

"Please, be serious. Now that you've read all about your family, are you going to share with me?"

"Share? Share what, Maggie? You've already made up your mind about everything."

"No, I haven't. I mean, I thought I knew what it meant, but now I'm not sure about anything."

Emma pointed to all the books, the desks overflowing with papers and notebooks. "All of this information here and yet you were so evasive right from the moment we met."

"What could I say to you, Emma? How could I say I am living a legacy a few hundred years old and it will kill me? Why would anyone believe me about such things?"

"I would have believed you."

"No, you wouldn't. You've already said it's all nonsense. Besides, what was I supposed to think? You appeared out of the blue, and given our families' histories, I had to assume you knew everything and were going to be a willing instrument in my future, or lack of one."

Emma nodded. It made sense. "Is that why you waited for me down by the gatehouse?"

"In part." Maggie bit her lower lip. "I admit, I was curious about you."

"So then all of this friendship a ruse?"

Maggie shook her head. "When I say I was expecting you, I wasn't talking about any Tapper. I was expecting *you*, and no one else."

"You didn't know who I was."

Maggie blushed. "I've seen you before," she said, and tapped the side of her head. "I've dreamed about you. Many times. Just in here. And I have stared into your eyes for hours."

"I see."

"Do you think me quite mad?"

Emma didn't answer straight away; there was nothing she could think to say. "Did you keep records of all the strangeness?"

"No, not at first. Not until we—my family, that is—realized what was going on. By then, several generations of bad luck had been and gone. After that, it was too late to look back with any certainty."

"I can see how that could happen," Emma admitted.

"Do you trust me? Do you trust me enough to tell me your secrets?"

"I have always trusted you, Maggie. Always." She shook her head. "But you have never trusted me, have you? You still don't."

"It isn't that. I knew you would come, and I feared you. Yet you're different from the person I expected."

"Is that a good thing?"

"Yes. I can talk to you. You are the first Tapper that anyone in my family could talk to. I think that's real progress."

Emma smiled, "Talking makes it all easier."

"It does, so what did you mean about Emily Tapper?"

"All right then, did you know that Emily had a sister? A twin sister?"

"What? Where does that come from?"

"From my papers. According to these records, Emily had a twin sister. A mirror twin they called her, because although they looked identical, some things were mirrored. Emily was left-handed, but her sister, Emma, was right-handed."

"A twin!" Maggie exclaimed. "I didn't know she had a twin."

"Not many people did. It was kept quiet, and then over time it became a part of the lost history."

"Emma and Emily, then. You were named after the other twin?"

"I don't think it was intentional, Maggie."

"Maybe it was. Maybe your parents knew you would come back to claim your inheritance one day."

"Why?"

"They would want a Tapper to witness my demise."

"No." Emma shook her head vehemently. "I really don't think so." She couldn't be absolutely sure if her biological parents knew anything or not. "I think it's all just a coincidence. Emma is a nice name, and there is nothing more to it than that."

"Do you think, in a world where the supernatural is not only possible but exists for real, that there are truly such things as coincidences?"

Emma thought for a moment. "All right. There are too many strange things here to rely on chance."

"That said, you're here. You see all our history in this room, and there is no mention of anything like this. I have read through all our records."

"You don't have access to the Tapper family notes. They're private and personal journals and they go all the way back to John Tapper, Emily's father. He was so incensed about his daughter Emily's treatment and death that he charged a priest to write it all down. All of the Tappers have maintained the records ever since. They would never forget what happened to her."

"And is it as I feared, that they killed Emily and took her child as their own?"

"No," Emma answered.

"So I am not Emily's descendant?"

Emma shook her head. "No. I told you."

Maggie's relief was almost visible. "Thank goodness."

Emma grinned. "Oh my world, you thought that we were related didn't you?"

"Distantly, yes, probably."

"You should have looked at the eyes, if you were related to Emily Tapper don't you think someone in your family tree would have had brown eyes too?"

Maggie grinned, "good point."

"Now you are certain we're not related does this mean you'll stop backing away from me?"

"I don't want to back away. I never did, but I didn't want to hurt you, either."

"You wouldn't."

"And there's still this curse of Emily Tapper." Maggie frowned, "Now that you're here, I feel it will all happen sooner rather than later."

"Rubbish. You are not going to die young, and no curse will take you. I won't allow it," Emma said.

"You won't allow it?"

"No. Look, our families are linked, and although they may only be related by tragedy, but if we can figure this out, then the curse will stop, too."

Maggie shook her head. "'Related by tragedy.' You make it sound so straightforward."

"It is, really. Think about it. Emily And Charles had an affair, and he dumped her when she got pregnant. Emily would not be the first woman to succumb to the charms of a more privileged man." Emma said. "And she will not be the last to be the one vilified for it, either."

"Not something anyone has to worry about with me," Maggie said.

"You could charm me."

"I thought I already had."

"Yes, Magwood Durrant. You have."

"Then what?"

"Then Emily lost her life and the life of her baby, I don't have the details of how."

"What about Emma? Where does she come into this?"

"She'd been placed in fosterage – if that's the right word – and went straight into maid service as soon as she could. She didn't even stay in Castlecoombe."

"What next?" Maggie asked.

They both stared at the oversized tree for inspiration. Maggie's hand sought Emma's, and their fingers entwined. "What do you want from me, Maggie?"

"Everything."

"You already have everything I can give," Emma said.

"I'm not sure I deserve you, Emma Tapper."

"Not Tapper, Blewitt," Emma corrected. "Believe in yourself, and we can make this work out for us."

"Good, because I have nothing without you in my life. You know, I thought if we could reconcile our differences, then maybe Emily would forgive me."

"So it *was* all a ruse. You just want the feud to end?"

"I want the feud to end, of course, but what we have, you and I, is not a ruse."

"I know. Do you think it can be fixed?"

"I have no idea. I would do anything."

"To save your life?"

"To be with you." She waved her hand with dramatic flourish. "Everything you see here is window dressing. Decorations of a life I do not value, and I would give it all away in an instant."

"What do you want?" Emma repeated.

"I want to live. I want to spend time with you. I want to enjoy what I have with you."

"What do you want to do about it?"

Maggie didn't need to think about it. "I'll give it all to my brother. My title, holdings, everything, and I will leave here and go with you to the city, if you would have me."

"Are you serious? You would give this up?"

"In a shot."

Emma stared out of narrowed eyes. "Is it to escape the wrath of the ghost?"

"It doesn't work like that. One way or another, Emily will take her due. Rueben Durrant," Maggie said, pointing to a name halfway down the tree, "thought he was above all this, so he moved away. Left the estates to his brother and moved to a vineyard in Italy."

"What happened?"

"They found him in bed, wrapped in wet bedsheets, his throat bearing the marks of someone hanged." She shrugged. "If you're the firstborn and it's your time, then you're done. No matter where you are when it happens."

Emma paused. "Swift. The body—they said he was strangled?"

"I thought he'd been killed by the ghost."

"The ghost of Emily Tapper?"

"Yes. I don't know why, unless she was protecting what was, or is, hers, as she sees it. As far as I know she only kills the firstborn."

"Right. What do you want to do, Maggie?"

"Let's leave here. Tonight."

"It won't solve your problems though, will it?"

"I know, but I don't know what else to do."

"We need to think of a way to solve this, not run away."

"Until she forgives the Magwoods, there can be no peace. I would rather enjoy what we have in the time I have left." The words caught in her throat.

"I'm not ready to let you go so soon."

Maggie gripped Emma's hand tightly. "I don't think there is anything we can do."

"What do *you* think happened to Emily?"

"It's hard to know for sure, no one noted how or why it all started. No one cared, I suppose. There have been rumors and speculation, but nothing more than that."

"And that's all you have?" Emma waved her sheaf of papers about like a weapon. "My records say Charles murdered Emily and her baby, and then hanged her on the tree to make it look like suicide. Her last words to her father were, 'Charles will accept this child as his, and name him as his own son, or pay the price for all time.'"

"I see." Maggie looked thoughtful.

"See? See what, Maggie? What do you know?"

"There was a rumor."

"You've been holding back."

She flushed. "No, and before you get mad at me, hear me out. As I said, there was a rumor, but it didn't amount to much. It does now."

"Well, come on. The suspense is killing me."

"You remember how the steps up here were cold?"

"And wet."

"Yes, indeed. Well, the cold has always been there, but it gets worse."

"Like now?"

Maggie nodded. "That's part of the ghost effect. You know, the cold from beyond the grave. But the water is different. It only started a few weeks or so ago."

"About the time I arrived?"

"Give or take, yes. The rumor, one of many, was written in an old journal. It suggested Charles Senior sent his son away, and when Emily came to confront the son, she met the father and his wife instead. Legend has it they pushed her down the stairs of the east turret—"

"This one?"

"Indeed. Then, in the dark of the night, they dragged her to the tree to hang like a suicide. Suicide was such an evil and ungodly thing then, and everyone wished to forget the whole thing as quickly as possible for fear the taint would affect other members of the community."

"What about the baby?" Emma asked.

"Some say the baby was taken away, never to be seen in Castlecoombe. Others say that meant they killed the baby, whilst others say there was no baby at all."

"But what do you think happened?"

"One way or another, I think my ancestors killed them both."

"So how can we persuade the ghost of Emily Tapper to forgive you for what Charles Senior did?"

"I'm thinking about it," Maggie answered. "I'm thinking."

"Think faster."

"Seriously, Emma. In all the books I've read, the ghost will never be satisfied, and the curse will continue until someone undoes what was done. How the hell am I supposed to undo something an ancestor did a few hundred years ago?"

"You'll think of something."

28

LEAVING

Emma yawned. "I know you wanted to leave tonight, but it's late. I haven't packed anything, and I don't like the idea of traveling through the mountains in the dark. Not again."

Maggie glanced at her watch and groaned. It was already past midnight. Time was already too short. "We need to go now. I have a bad feeling about this."

"Why? We can go first thing in the morning, when it's light and we can see. Also we've been drinking, and that's never a good idea."

"It's already too late," Maggie said. She cocked her head to the side. "Listen."

On the chest of drawers near the wall, a clock ticked its way to the quarter hour. With each *tick-tock*, the sound seemed louder, more defined.

They turned to the door and rushed for it as it burst open and slammed shut with a rush of cold air. More cloudy gusts wafted into the room from the small gap at the bottom. Ice crystals settled on the ground, and the white frost of extreme cold crept over the wooden planks.

"Do you?" a voice echoed around the tower.

"What?" asked Emma. "What did you say?"

"That wasn't me," Maggie replied.

Emma stepped closer to her and held on to her arm.

"Do. You?"

"Is that…?"

"Yes. She's here now."

"This is where it gets bad, isn't it?" Emma asked, but Maggie didn't respond. "How bad will it get? What do we do?"

"I don't know. I've never been in this room with a Tapper before."

"I'm not–"

"Yes, you are, no matter your name."

A breeze, cold and bitter, circled around the women. *"Maagwood,"* whispered the distant voice.

"She knows your name."

"No, we are all Magwood to her."

"It is time. I come for you."

"Damn," Maggie mumbled.

"No more…Magwood."

A woman, small and petite, wearing a stained white gown, walked out of the cold breeze as though walking through a doorway to another place. Her clothes, her skin, even her long dark hair and eyes that should have been black as coal, all blazed with a stark inner fire. She was alight with a radiant eerie green that reflected on the ice upon the floor.

Around her throat, a thick band of rust red glistened in the poor light, and from her shoulders, a congealed blue-green slime oozed over her gown. A rope, thick and befouled with who knew what, hung about her neck in sinuous loops.

"Get behind me," Maggie ordered. "She's come for me. You don't need to be hurt as well."

"Magwood." Wind raced round the room and grew faster and more violent closer to the ghost. Yet, at the very heart of

those winds, Emily Tapper stood in absolute stillness, untouched by the raging gusts.

She stared at Maggie. *"Dooo you?"*

"I have no idea what you mean." She looked at Emma. "I don't know what to say."

Emma smiled and stepped forward. "Emily," she said. "Emily, *look* at me." For a moment, the shade turned. Her black eyes, dark and distant, glared at Emma, considered her presence, then ignored her. "That worked well," Emma said.

"Hide," Maggie tried again. "Escape, if you can. Once she has me, she will not harm you."

"No." Emma stated, with more bravery than she felt. "I am Emma Tapper," she said even more loudly, "and I will not run from family."

"Emma?" The figure stopped moving, even the force of the winds lessened.

"Do you not recognize me, Emily? Your own kin."

"Emma…" she whispered, and the word raced across the room as though borne on a chill breeze.

"Please, Emma," Maggie cried out. "Don't do this. Get away, now, before it is too late."

Emma grabbed Maggie's hand. "It's already too late."

The ghost looked at the two of them, and rage washed out in waves of ice. *"No,"* she hissed. *"Never again."* A pale, green-tinged hand reached out. *"No Magwood. Never again."* The rope around her neck snaked along Emily's arm and shot from her open hand.

Maggie tried to move, but the rope whipped around her neck and tightened too quickly for her to dodge. She fell to her knees with a strangled cry, and with a loud *thwack*, the rope tightened until her voice cut off.

She was helpless to do anything about it.

"Maggie!" Emma cried out, and the sound of her voice echoed around the quiet tower.

Maggie looked terrified. Her eyes bulged as the rope cut

into her skin. She clawed at the ever-tightening noose, until she grew so desperate her fingers dug into her flesh.

Emma fell to her knees and tried to help, but the rope was too tight and the ghost's strength and resolve too great.

"Be strong, Maggie," she whispered. "Hold on for me."

A woman scorned, she remembered.

She rose to her feet and pulled back her shoulders. "Emily Tapper," she said, and her voice wavered so much she wasn't sure she heard herself, never mind the ghost.

It was not enough to make Emily pause.

"Stop!" she shouted at the top of her voice. "Emily Tapper, stop this right now!"

Eyes almost black and rimmed with red turned in her direction. It was a start.

"Listen to me. I am Emma Tapper, daughter of Emma Tapper, your sister." Emily didn't move, although it seemed she paused to listen. It was not enough to keep her attention, and she turned her dark and doleful awareness back to Maggie.

"That worked a treat," she mumbled to herself. Think. Think. Think.

"Mother!" Emma roared with all the defiance of an enraged teenager. "Stop it!"

Emily turned toward Emma. The rope around Maggie's neck stopped tightening. *My child?* she whispered. *My Emma? My sweet, sweet Emma? Where are you, my baby?*

"Mother, I'm all grown up now."

"Grown?"

"Yes. I was saved."

"Oh, praise the heavens."

"My father saved me."

"Charles! Dirty, evil, conniving bastard."

"Yes, mother," Emma said. "But you're killing my Magwood, and she is mine. Not yours."

"Yours?"

"Mine."

"Mine."

"No, mine." Emma repeated. She knelt before Maggie and smiled until it hurt her teeth. "Magwood, I forgive you for all you have done. I forgive you. Will you do all that you must to put it right?"

Maggie stared but her lips were losing color.

"Noooooooo. You must not."

"Yes, mother, we will."

The rope around Maggie's neck loosened, and she took several deep gulps of precious air.

"Speak, Maggie," Emma instructed. "Say something to stop this."

"Like what?" Maggie croaked through her damaged throat.

"Imagine you're Charles and I'm Emily. What would you say to put it right?"

Maggie looked perplexed, but only for a moment. She smiled as she looked into Emma's eyes. "Marry me," she croaked. "I wronged you, and now I would put it right. Be my wife and take your place at Magwood Hall. You will be the Lady Magwood, as is your right."

The rope, looped around her neck, vanished. Emily stepped closer and her eyes softened. *"Do you?"* her disembodied voice echoed around the turret. *"Do you love her?"*

"Yes," Maggie looked into the face of the ghost, and her gaze did not waver. "I do, and now I understand."

The ghost nodded. *"I accept your will, my daughter."* Then she vanished. The air warmed, the ice crystals vanished, and normality–if such a thing could exist in Magwood Hall —resumed.

"Has she gone?" rasped Maggie. "Are we safe now?"

"Yes."

"Are you sure?" Maggie cocked her head to one side, as though she were trying to hear something. It was quiet, though, apart from the ticking of the clock and the *plink plink* of melted ice as it dropped from the door frame to the floor. Maggie blew out a long breath, but the chill had vanished and her breath no longer steamed.

"Yes, I think so," Emma said.

"It's quiet. There are no strange sounds. The baby's cries have ended and the chill has gone."

"It's all quite ordinary and mundane."

"Finally," Maggie said. "I think you might be right."

"Do you still want to leave tonight?"

Maggie cleared her throat. "I'm exhausted. I want to go to bed and sleep."

"Me, too." Emma looked at the Durrant and Magwood family tree on the wall and thought about what she wanted to say. "Did you mean what you said to Emily?"

Maggie nodded and held out her hand. "Yes, I did."

"You don't have to say it now. It worked. She's gone."

Maggie shook her head. "I spoke truth, and even though she's gone, I think I'd like to know that Emily is always there, looking out for you."

"I suppose we don't have to leave now."

"We don't have to, I know. But I said I would leave all of this and go home with you. I still would."

"You're prepared to turn your back on everything and everyone?"

"I promised I would to keep you safe and live a normal life. I will do what I can for everyone here, of course. I would not leave them at the mercy of my brother, not without some protections. But other than looking after the people who live here, I think it's time to leave this all behind and think of our future."

"If you're sure this is what you want?"

"It is. It would be nice to have the time to get to know you properly."

"Then we'll leave first thing in the morning," Emma said.

29

DEAR CHARLES

Charles Durrant sat before the fire in the great hall and couldn't stop grinning to himself. All that time he'd spent trying to plan his sister's death, and it would have been faster and easier to find her a pretty girlfriend. He shook his head and sipped his glass of fine malt whiskey. It was good to be home. His home.

All his.

That Weasel chap had made such a mess of things, getting himself killed like that. Thank goodness, he himself had been caught on video at an all-night poker game. It had been a good game, too. He hadn't even lost any money.

He raised his glass. "A toast to fortune and inheritance," he said. He took a sip of his drink, took a deep, satisfied breath, and shivered.

He grabbed another log from the pile and threw it into the fire. He watched as the log caught and eventually started to burn, but that didn't make the room any warmer. As he breathed, he saw the steam of his breath on the air. Yet no matter how close he stood next to the fire, he couldn't get warm.

Somewhere in the hall, he heard the sound of solid heels

hitting stone floors, like the stairs, or the kitchen. *Click-clack, clickity-clack.*

Charles grabbed the poker from the side of the fireplace and gripped it tightly.

Click-clack, clickity-clack.

"What the hell?" He stormed across the hall, poker in hand, and opened the door to the kitchen.

Click-clack, clickity-clack.

The temperature dropped even further. Every breath erupted from his mouth in bursts of steam. He gripped the poker even tighter, as though that would fend off the chill.

"Who's there?" he shouted. "Show yourself."

No one answered.

Behind him, a distant and wavering voice asked, *"Do you?"*

"What the hell?" he responded. "Who the hell is there?" He spun around and stalked back into the hall, but he saw no one. One by one, the windows froze over and letters appeared in the icy windows.

'DO. YOU?'

The letters looked ill-formed, but they were legible. A moment later, they were gone, replaced by more ice. Charles stared at the windows for a moment, then he spun on his heels and ran toward the door. His heart pounded so hard, he thought his chest would burst.

The door slammed shut in his face.

"Do you?" the voice asked.

He leaned his back against the closed door. His gaze darted from side to side. "Who are you?" he asked in a weak and trembling voice.

"Do you?" the voice asked again, and when he tracked the sound, he saw a woman. She looked pale, almost transparent, and radiated a strange green light. She had dark hair and eyes like pools of midnight.

"Do you?" she repeated. When he didn't reply, she floated in his direction. A long, discolored rope that looped around her neck also looped around her arms and her body.

"Revenge is mine. The Magwood must die."

Charles knew exactly what she meant then. "I'm not the Magwood. I am Charles–"

"Charlesssss," the ghost interrupted. She grinned, a wide, hideous grin that allowed her blackened tongue to loll out to the side.

Charles screamed. He didn't stop until the slime-covered rope wrapped around his neck and tightened until he could barely breath. The ghost of Emily Tapper dragged him across the hall to the center of the room.

She stood inches before him and asked, *"Where's my baby?"*

Charles fell to his knees and sobbed through the constriction around his throat. "I…I don't know."

A chair dragged itself across the floor and stopped inches away from him. The rope around his neck tightened and pulled him upward until he stood on the chair. Only then did the grip lessen, but if he didn't stand upright, the rope choked him.

"The Lady Magwood wants things just right…" she said. A breeze that had no place inside the building sprang up. It grew more forceful until the wind, with the strength of a gale, roared around the room. Dust and small items sucked up into the winds dashed against him with such force he had to cover his face to protect himself. Furniture, even the large and heavy items, rearranged themselves, until the center of the room had emptied of everything except Charles on the chair.

"Do you?" she asked.

The rope tightened around his neck and pulled him upward. He rose up on tiptoe, but the tightened rope still cut off his air. He tried to hold on to it, to make it slacken a bit to keep from suffocating, but he put too much pressure on the side of the chair, and it fell over.

Charles swung from his neck for a moment. He thought this was it; it was time to die. Then she let go, and he fell to the floor in a heap. He pulled at the rope until it loosened enough that he could breathe. His throat hurt, his head pounded, and his heart had nearly burst.

"What...what...do you want?" he asked. He received no answer, and when he looked up, she wasn't there.

"Fuck!" He scrambled to his feet and rushed toward the hallway. He'd left his car keys in the kitchen, so he slunk across the hallway as quietly as possible. He got as far as the kitchen door when all the lights went out. Except for the ghost. She glowed even brighter now that there were no other lights.

"Charlesssss. It is time."

As she spoke, Charles noticed the ticking of the old clock.

Tick. Tock. But then, the moment between the tick and the tock seemed to lengthen as the temperature in the kitchen dropped. All at once, the knives in the knife block rose into the air. They stayed hanging there, points up as though waiting for something.

Time lengthened.

Tick.

Charles had never noted such a weird dilation of the clock. A teapot floated high into the air and shattered.

Tock.

He fell to his knees and covered his head. "Please, let me go."

Tick.

The *whoosh* of something, a knife, flying through the air

made him duck down even more. He shuddered when all the knives *thudded* into the wood.

Tock.

Charles didn't move. He thought if he could make himself small enough and ignore it, then she would go away.

"Charles," she said. *"Look."*

Tick.

When he stood up, he tried to put the table between them. She yanked on the rope that was still around his neck and drew him closer.

She'd gouged words into the wood. Two words. 'Puppet master.' It looked as though she had started to write more but decided against it. The ghost pointed at the word and then at him. *"Charles."*

Silence filled the kitchen. He couldn't hear the usual sounds, like the hiss of the refrigerators.

He jumped, though, when the clock started to work with a loud *tick, tock.*

There were no delays.

"I am not a–"

"Murderer!" she squawked. The rope tightened around his neck again, and she pulled at him with such force, he fell over.

He lost one shoe as she dragged him up the stairs. He caught his jacket on something on the way to the east tower, and as she kept going, the nice, expensive jacket ripped. She dragged him into the old stairwell up to the east turret, his sister's domain, and they stopped on a small landing near the door. Dampness covered the steps and the wall.

"Do you?"

The other end of the rope snaked upward and wrapped over an exposed beam above the stairs. With little apparent effort, the ghost pulled until Charles dangled a foot in the air. No matter how hard he struggled, the rope would neither loosen from the beam, nor let him breath. He danced at the end of the rope, and the ghost watched with cold, black eyes before she tied the rope so he hung there.

She ripped his clothes apart and, with a knife he never knew she had, ripped him across the belly.

"Am I a suitable match now, Magwood?" she asked.

She walked away from him, down the stairs, *click-clack, clickity-clack,* and disappeared from view.

She reappeared as the darkness closed in around his eyes. As he clung to life and wished it would end.

"It's time, Charles. A Tapper will walk these halls, and my revenge will last forever."

She grabbed his legs and pulled hard.

30

TROUBLE AT THE HALL

P hil Jackson stepped out of the pub and pulled his jacket collar up as the cold weather made him shiver. It was a vile night. The wind was up, and although the rain had not yet started, he smelled it on the air. The storm hadn't arrived, but it would, and Castlecoombe would again be battered by rain and high wind. It was why they were all at the pub so late. There'd be no work in the morning except clean up. All the animals were inside the barn, safe, and the farm would stay secure, as it always was.

He looked up as Judy joined him. "Would you be taking a look at that!" she said, and pointed.

Phil looked along the valley, to the manor perched over it. "Good grief," he said, as flash after flash of lightning lit the castle walls with stark brightness. Lights from within the house flashed on and off. Then they all came on, every single one, from the forty-six-bulb chandelier in the formal dining room to every light upstairs and downstairs. Phil knew something was amiss. "Maggie needs our help."

"Lord Magwood ain't here. She ran off with the Tapper girl, remember?"

"Maybe she came back," he said.

His wife shrugged. "We should let them be. It's not for us to intrude in the ways of lords and their affairs."

"This is Lord Magwood, our Maggie, we're talking about. The one who gives us jobs we can do and rent we can afford. Maggie always did us a good turn," he said.

"I know. I worry for her, you know I do. But that family has always been a weird lot."

"I'm still worried for her."

"No matter what I say, you're going to take a look, aren't you?"

He smiled grimly. "I must."

Judy's eyes turned to the strange effects up at the hall, then back to her husband. "I'll not have you go up there alone. I'll ask them in the pub to come give you a hand. If Maggie needs help, we ought to be the ones who give it. Like you said, she's been good to us."

Phil raced to his Land Rover, and given that the rather temperamental engine usually needed a few attempts to get started, he was surprised when he turned the key and the engine roared to life on the first attempt. Other men of the town raced out of the pub and jumped into the back of the vehicle. Some even sat on the hard top. There was no need for words; they could see there was trouble. Maggie needed them.

As they drove up the hill, a whole convoy of villagers drove or walked behind them. No one rushed into the house. Helping was one thing, but a headlong hurry into the madness inside was something very different.

They stopped, as one, when the lightning struck. They stared as a woman in a long white robe, glowing green and blue, danced above the tower, swinging in some weird dance with the lightning rod atop the roof. Some reached for their mobile phones and called emergency services. When the log pile at the back of the courtyard burst into flames, the men raced back there and used whatever they could to douse them.

"Don't go inside," Phil's wife urged.

Of all the villagers, only three went inside the house. Phil Jackson was one of them. When they came out, not one would say a word about what they'd found inside.

"What's going on?" Judy asked.

"Best not to ask," Phil said. He looked at the other villagers. "Best go home. Call the police before we lose the telephones. Tell them there's lightning, and fires, and maybe someone is hurt."

"Is there?" Judy persisted.

"We'll leave that to the emergency services," he said. "Now, folks, go home and make the calls. I'll be the only one here. I'll be letting the police know."

31

IN THE CITY

It was quite strange for Maggie to move from a large rambling house with lots of open space into a small flat with no outdoor space at all. They had a tiny balcony, but it was so small it didn't count for much. Miles and miles of tarmac and concrete spread out in all directions, and what little nature existed was bare and forlorn.

Autumn had arrived early, and it brought so many storms, the winds stripped the leaves from what few trees remained. Grasses, stomped by thousands of feet, now looked more like squares of mud than grass. Gone, too, were the sounds of the birds at dawn, replaced by car engines, beeping horns, and the not-too-distant rattle of the subway.

Security was also something she hadn't considered much of the time in Castlecoombe, and three weeks after moving to the city, Emma still needed to remind her to bolt doors and check identity tags before opening the door to anyone. At Castlecoombe, she would have opened any door without a second thought, and those doors she'd left unlocked all day anyway. Thoughts of the open spaces, the mountains, and the fields often intruded on her thoughts, but she had promised to turn her back on Castlecoombe and would continue to do so.

Even here, in the city, without a job or anything worthwhile to do, she still woke earlier than Emma. It was due to the noise as much as anything. How anyone could sleep through the perpetual racket was impossible to know.

Emma had quit her job the moment they'd arrived in the city, but she had her own money and didn't need another one for a while. She'd said she would find a better one and then maybe they could see about moving to the suburbs or something. The worst part about being here, Maggie thought, was that she had nothing, and no job either, to contribute to the household.

When the doorbell rang, Maggie remembered to look through the peephole to see who was there before she unlocked the door. When she realized who stood outside, she ignored the temptation to ignore them. Instead, she opened the door. The police, she knew, wouldn't stop bothering her until they said what they came to say.

"Detective Tallins and Detective Peters, what a joyful surprise to see you here," she said.

"Miss Durrant," Tallins said.

She looked at her watch. "I think you'll find even the dawn chorus is abed at this hour, so I cannot see why you would be surprised to find me home. How are you here at this hour?"

"We set off early," Tallins answered.

"Yes, you must have. You are a very long way from home."

"Can we come inside?" Peters asked.

Maggie stood in the doorway and blocked them. "Why? What is it you think I've done this time?"

"Nothing," Tallins soothed, "but this would be better discussed inside."

"Why?"

"It would be more comfortable."

"For you, or for me?" She did not wait for an answer, but turned her back on them and strode into the lounge. She settled herself in an armchair and waited for them to speak.

Emma came out of the bathroom, her hair still wet from the shower, and stopped to see who the visitors were before she perched on the armrest of Maggie's chair. "Detectives," she said, and nodded at them.

"Miss Blewitt. Miss Durrant," Peters started, "there has been an incident—"

"Incident? Do you mean an accident? What sort of accident?" Maggie demanded.

He frowned at the interruption.

"At Magwood Hall…" His voice trailed off, and Tallins took over.

"Miss Durrant, there was a fatal incident involving your brother, Charles Durrant."

"What? How?"

"We are still investigating the circumstances of the—"

"To hell with your investigation, what happened to my brother?" Maggie thundered. She glared at the detectives, but her stomach churned and her heart pounded. She took comfort in Emma's hand upon her shoulder, but that didn't stop the world from spinning.

"You'd better start at the beginning," Emma said. "Tell us everything."

Tallins nodded. "As you may have noticed, over the last few days, much of the country has been battered by storms."

Maggie and Emma nodded. Even in the city, it was hard to avoid the power of the weather.

"Castlecoombe was no exception. Tuesday evening—"

"Three days ago?"

Peters nodded, and Tallins continued. "We received several calls from concerned residents." He paused. "There were fires, flashing lights, and bolts of lightning that went up and down the towers and all around the hall."

"There were twenty-seven calls that all said pretty much the same thing. The castle was flashing so bright, the villagers thought the castle itself was causing the lightning," Peters said. "Emergency services dispatched two fire engines in case the electrical disturbance caused a fire, ambulances for any injuries, and of course a squad car also attended in case they were needed."

"All of the emergency services searched the house until they found Charles. We were led to believe he'd hanged himself in one of the stairwells, and that's where we found him. I'm sorry," Tallins added.

Maggie sat back in her chair and stroked Emma's hand on her shoulder.

"As a result, we are treating his death as suspicious, I'm afraid," Peters said.

"Surely you don't think I had anything to do with it?"

Neither man smiled. Neither responded. "We would like you to come and identify him, as his next of kin. There are also a few things we'd like you to look over."

Maggie looked from one detective to another. "Charles is really dead? No, that can't be."

Detective Peters nodded. "It looks like a vicious and violent break in. The Hall is a mess—well, parts of it are. We'll also need you to take an inventory and list anything you think might have been stolen."

"Okay," she mumbled. "There's a full inventory of everything with the insurance company. Anything else is irrelevant."

"We can provide transport, if you like."

"We'll drive back to Castlecoombe ourselves," Emma said. "I won't rely on anyone else to get us home afterward."

32
_____

THE END?

Cold, sterile light filled the waiting room with a glare so bright it seared Maggie's eyes. Emma sat at her side and held her hand in support. Maggie was grateful she was here. Next to the doors, the detectives stood like a pair of impassive stone guardians, eyes ahead, fixed and unfocused.

A man in a white lab coat opened the door and inclined his head a fraction toward them. "Whenever you're ready, Miss Durrant," he said, his voice as bland as his face.

Maggie didn't move at first, but Emma got to her feet and helped Maggie stand. "It will be all right," she whispered. "I'm here with you. Take your time."

"I'm okay," Maggie said. And she was, until she saw his face, peaceful and sneer-free. Now, he looked like the carefree young man he should have been rather than the bitter brother he had become. "That's him," she said in a quiet voice. "That's Charles, my brother."

"Thank you," said Detective Tallins.

She nodded. "I should make arrangements..."

Emma gripped Maggie's hand. "We can sort those out later."

"Will you be going to Magwood Hall today?" Peters asked.

"No," Emma answered for her. "We'll go to my house first and grieve. Perhaps we'll go for a drink at the local."

"Very well. There are some things we'd like to go through with you, shall I arrange transport from Maud's house up to the hall? Say nine a.m. tomorrow. If that's all right with you?" Peters asked.

Emma nodded, but Maggie didn't seem to care. "Fine," Emma said, "but right now, I think someone needs a good stiff drink."

She drove the rest of the way from Moorville to Castlecoombe. Maggie didn't care too much, not even when she folded herself into the tiny little city car Emma drove. On the way, Maggie didn't say a word and Emma didn't impose for a second. She was pleased about that. She needed to think.

"We're here," Emma said.

Maggie looked up at Maud's house, but she didn't move.

"Come on, sweetheart." Emma raced around and helped her out of the car.

"I'm fine," Maggie insisted. "I can manage."

"Of course you can," Emma said. "Come on in, and let's have a cuppa, shall we?"

"I was thinking of something stronger," Maggie said, as they went inside the house.

"A cup of tea first, to warm you up. How about you get the fire started while I put the kettle on."

Maggie nodded. "All right."

By the time Emma returned with two mugs of tea, Maggie had the fire lit, and it roared with a bright life. It would take some time to add much heat to the room, but she could already feel the change in temperature.

"Come sit at the table," Emma said.

"At the table?"

"Yes. We need to eat something."

"I'm not hungry," Maggie said.

"You need to eat."

Emma stared into her eyes until Maggie relented.

"All right," she said.

"Good. Sit with me on the sofa, then. I've made you a tea sweetened with honey. You'll feel better afterward." She pressed the cup into Maggie's cool, stiff fingers. "Drink."

She stayed for a while, maybe to make sure she drank some of the tea, and then Emma left her to go into the kitchen. Maggie heard her moving in the small space. When she returned, she put a warm plate on Maggie's knees. Maggie stared at the poached eggs on toast. "I'm not–"

"I know. You said, but you need to eat. This is plain and simple and easy to digest. Now, eat."

Maggie took a mouthful of food, chewed a few times, and swallowed. Emma did the same. She continued without much appetite until they were done.

"Finished," Maggie said, and placed her empty plate on the coffee table.

"Then it's time for a strong drink, now that you have some food inside you."

"Emma," Maggie started, "do we have to go to the local for a drink?"

"No, sweetheart, we can stay here."

"Good. I'm not in the mood."

Emma got to her feet and left the room, taking the empty dishes with her. She returned a few minutes later with a bottle of brandy and two glasses. "Maud had all kinds of things in her pantry. She just happened to have a bottle of this. It's not good brandy, though."

"It will do," Maggie said.

Emma poured two glasses and sat on the sofa next to Maggie. "Here you are, take this," she said. She pressed one of the glasses into her hand.

"I seem to be pretty useless today," Maggie said.

"You've had a big shock."

"Yes," Maggie agreed. She took a good mouthful of her drink and swallowed. Then she coughed. "That's dreadful stuff."

"Is it?"

"Yes. Give me another shot."

Emma refilled Maggie's glass, then pulled her against her side and wrapped an arm around her shoulders. It felt good to cuddle up together.

"Thank you," Maggie said.

"For?"

"Being here."

Emma smiled and held her closer. "I'll always be here."

"Tomorrow as well?"

"Tomorrow, and all the tomorrows after that, if you want."

"Yes."

M aggie didn't say a word when Detectives Tallins and Peters pulled up outside Maud's house. At least they didn't bang on the door again. She would have preferred to walk up the hill. Right then, she didn't want to answer to anyone. But there were so many cars and vans coming and going, the walk would not have been a safe one. It was better to be in a police car rather than keep stopping to explain who they were.

At the house, the forensics and crime scene teams were still wandering around, carrying things in plastic bags and plastic boxes, filling trays and cartons, and fitting them inside small white vans.

Maggie and Emma were ushered through the front door and back to the kitchen. At first glance, it looked normal enough, but as soon as they walked in, Maggie realized things were not how or where they should be.

All of the kitchenware had been thoroughly displaced: the

pots and pans no longer hanging on the wall, but stacked neatly on the wrong shelves; kitchen implements taken from their places next to the stove and placed in neat order on a side cabinet.

There were breakages, though, with the table covered in tiny shards of china, pottery, and plastic. These things weren't just smashed but looked as though they had exploded. If she could think of any natural reason for such destruction, then it would be as though a hurricane had blown through the place.

"What a mess," she said. She didn't say anything about the rearrangement of pots. What would that matter to the police?

"Once we're done, a cleanup crew will come and sort everything out," Tallins said.

"And when will that be?" she asked.

"First thing in the morning if that is acceptable."

"Fine." Although that meant even more strangers in her house.

Her escorts led her towards the cellar steps, and Maggie closed her eyes. Her heart beat a little faster, but she composed herself carefully. "Here? Again?" she asked, her eyes still closed.

"No, not again," Peters said,

"The writing on the door," Detective Tallins directed. "What do you make of it?"

Maggie opened her eyes and steeled herself for what she might see.

Etched into the wood and colored in rust red, crude letters formed the words:

'And to the puppet master, the debt is paid.'

M aggie looked away. She didn't want to pay too much attention to the dark marks on the door or on the floor. "I haven't a clue. Who is the puppet master?"

Tallins shook his head, silently.

"How about you? Do you know what this puppet master reference means?" Peters asked Emma.

"No idea, either."

He nodded. "All right. Come this way, please."

Maggie stopped to look at the old kitchen clock. It had run so sure and reliably for generations, and now it stood still, its hands stopped at a quarter after twelve. Maggie knew, with as much certainty as intuition would allow, this was the work of Emily.

In the east wing, they made their way to the east turret. Nothing seemed damaged or disturbed, except that a rope hung from the top of the stairs, outside the turret door. The ends of the rope, neatly cut, swung back and forth on the currents of warm air flowing in and out of the stairwell.

"Here?" Maggie croaked.

"Yes," Tallins answered. There was no more to be said. He pointed at letters painted on the wall in russet brown: 'Puppet Master.'

"What does that mean?" Maggie asked.

"I'd hoped you would know," Tallins answered.

"I don't," Maggie said. "Who found him?"

"Philip Jackson," he replied. "He was the one who called to report the situation."

Maggie stood there, silent and unmoving. No one disturbed her, not now. The door to her turret stood open, so she walked inside. It was just as she had left it, the night they met Emily.

"Is there anything else, detective?" Emma asked.

"Indeed, one more thing." Tallins marched them back down to the main hall and pointed. In the center of the room, a straight-backed chair, overturned, the leg broken, caught her attention. The whole room had been rearranged, with the furniture forming a huge circle along the outer edges. More rust on the carpet merged with the colors of the rug, and she wondered if it was blood.

"What do you make of the message?" Tallins asked.

At the end of the room stood a side table, over which the wall had been defaced with large, crude lettering. Maggie walked closer. Her eyes focused on the letters.

'A gift for my daughter.
Settlement of debt, in fullness paid.
Long may she live, the Lady Magwood.'

EPILOGUE

Maggie waited until everyone, apart from Emma, had left before she felt free enough to roam around her house. It was too difficult to see the rooms where they had lived—where he had lived—and the places where they had fought.

"I don't know what I'm supposed to do now," Maggie said.

"You don't have to do anything, not right now. Take some time," Emma said.

"I know. I just feel lost. I'm not at all sure what to make of this."

"You're the Lord of Magwood Hall again. Even Emily Tapper agrees. Long live the Lady Magwood."

She spun around to the message and then turned back to Emma. "But I'm not the Lady Magwood, Emma. I'm Lord Magwood. If you were my wife, then *you* would be the Lady Magwood."

"Oh." Emma's brows furrowed for a moment. "Then that settles it."

"What are you thinking?"

"You have responsibilities here, Maggie. To the hall, to the people of Castlecoombe, and to yourself."

"Yes. But—"

"And you don't like the city at all." Emma interrupted.

"Yes, that's true, but it's not just about me, is it? You need to be happy, too."

"Since I've met you, everything has changed. I don't need the city. There is nothing there for me. Everything I want is here, where you are. I can sell the city flat and move here. I have a house here, after all."

Maggie couldn't stop herself from smiling so hard it hurt. "Seriously? You would do that? Move to Castlecoombe"

Emma stared into her eyes. "I would. You just have to say that is what you want."

"I do. Very much. Maybe you'd like to stay with me in the hall."

"With all the Tapper portraits as well?"

"Yes, all them. The feud is over, and Emily Tapper gave us her blessing."

Maggie opened her arms, and when Emma stepped into her embrace and held on, she knew they were both home and safe. She kissed the top of Emma's head as thoughts turned toward the future.

"Maggie," Emma said.

She looked into Emma's Tapper eyes and smiled.

Emma stood on tiptoe and kissed Maggie on the mouth. "It's all over now. We're safe."

Maggie was about to agree when Emma silenced her with a kiss, and this one took all of her attention and promised a life full of such kisses.

I hope you have enjoyed this story. If you did, please consider leaving an honest review. It is the life blood of an author and makes us smile.
Most of all, I just want to know that you have enjoyed the story.

Thank you

If you want to know more about new books, background details and information not printed any place else, then subscribe to the reader's list.

https://www.subscribepage.com/nitaround

Visit my website at
www.nitaround.com

Or join my facebook group

www.facebook.com/groups/nitaroundbooks/

The Towers of the Earth

Prequel: A Pinch of Salt
Prequel: A Hint of Hope
Book 1: A Touch of Truth
Book 2: A Touch of Rage
Book 3: A Touch of Darkness
Book 4: A Touch of Ice

The Evie Chester Files:

Case 1: Lost and Found
Case 2: Sirens and Syphons
Case 3: Fur and Fangs

Stand Alone Stories

The Ghost of Emily Tapper

Romances as Encarnita Round

Fresh Start